ARLEEN ANDERSON had grown up in a small town, never knowing what poverty was. Suddenly she was thrust into one of the worst slum areas in the city of Saltboro, where she encountered:

Anna Luigi—who seemed to have no love for her children . . .

The Roosters—a gang of teenage boys who would do almost anything for thrills . . .

Neelie Ryan—a chronic bed patient who, in spite of her poverty and sickness, still had hope . . .

Arleen wanted to help these people although Dr. Mark Wynter, her roommate Evelyn, and a social worker told her that she could only mend their bodies, not their minds. But Arleen knew there was a way and she did everything she could to find it . . .

VISITING NURSE

Alice Brennan

WILDSIDE PRESS

Visiting Nurse

Published by Wildside Press LLC
www.wildsidepress.com

CHAPTER 1

WALKING BRISKLY down the cement path that led from the health department building where the Visiting Nurses Association was housed to the curb where her secondhand coupé was parked, Arleen Anderson grinned to herself. She pretended not to see the passing youth who had given out a piercing wolf whistle at the sight of her.

Once inside the little car, she turned the key in the switch. The motor started smoothly and purred like a kitten.

Arleen had picked up the car at a bargain price at a local secondhand automobile lot two months previously, just after she had come to Saltboro, a large industrial city, to work. The salesman, a balding sentimental man, had been moved by the sight of Arleen in the blue uniform and cape of the Visiting Nurses Association.

In the earlier days of the salesman's marriage, when money had been scarce and jobs few and far between, one of the visiting nurses had come every day for ten days to take care of his wife, who was bedridden with an infected leg. The nurse had even showed him how to care for his baby, who was only nine weeks old at the time.

So, to him, visiting nurses were only one notch below angels. He couldn't bring himself to let Arleen buy the car she had picked out.

"Listen, miss," he'd told her, keeping a wary eye toward the office and his boss, who certainly would not approve of his actions, "you don't want that car." He added quickly, at Arleen's puzzled look. "It's what we call a 'looker'—that means it looks fine outside, but it's a lemon. Now, if you want a really dependable car. . . ."

Arleen felt a tug of gratitude toward the salesman. After all the warnings she'd been given about how everyone was out to gyp you in the big city, she certainly had not found it like that at all.

The wolf whistle sounded again. Arleen did not turn her head as she steered the car out from the curb, but she was, womanlike, very much aware of the compliment the whistle implied. And, womanlike, she was pleased to be considered attractive enough to evince such a whistle.

Blue-eyed, with soft brown hair curling in pixie fashion around her slender face, she rarely failed to attract a second glance.

Her work this April morning took her into the Leland Street neighborhood. It was an area of narrow, ugly streets and cracked sidewalks, of curbside trash cans that served as places for small boys to sit, and as places to hide in some of their games. It was an area of crumbling brick apartment houses laced together by fire escapes; an almost windowless, dark jungle.

Arleen shuddered as she parked the car at the curb, picked up her nursing satchel and walked up to one of the buildings.

As soon as she had left the car, as if it was a cue for their appearance, a group of small children surrounded it, peeking and peering.

Arleen thought, "I should go back and lock the car." She'd been warned about Leland Street. "It's an area of vice and crime," she had been told. "We've never had any difficulty so far concerning our nurses, but we don't want to take chances. Be extremely careful not only of your possessions, Miss Anderson, but also of yourself."

Arleen hesitated. Perhaps she should lock the car. She half turned, and the children, again as if on cue, disappeared.

Arleen didn't return to the car. Instead, she walked up the cracked steps and inside the small, dark hall. There was no ventilation, and the hall smelled of damp and dust, stale food, cheap whiskey.

Arleen was appalled. Nothing in her conservative, middle-class life had prepared her for the ugliness and poverty of Leland Street.

After being graduated from nursing college, she had taken a course in public health nursing, and after that she had held down a job as a private nurse. But her patients had all belonged to the middle- or high-income group. Her work as visiting nurse was, for the first time, bringing to her the reality of how people outside her own social class lived.

She consulted her book. "Mrs. Alfred Ryan. Arthritic. Bedridden."

The Ryan apartment was on the fourth floor. Arleen plodded up the four flights of stairs. Her legs ached by the time she reached the upper hall.

She knocked at the door of the Ryan apartment and was

6

admitted at once by a short, unshaven man in a slightly soiled undershirt and blue slacks, baggy at the knees.

He scowled at her, his blue eyes antagonistic under thick, overhanging brows. "Whata you want?"

Arleen kept her voice soft and pleasant. "I'm the visiting nurse, Mr. Ryan."

A woman's voice called cheerfully from inside the room, "Let her in, Al. Mind your manners, now."

With no great show of graciousness, the man opened the door wide enough for Arleen to step inside the apartment, then slammed it shut behind her.

The "apartment" turned out to be one middle-sized room, serving as kitchen, bedroom, living room. It had one window facing the street. On the sill was a wooden box holding green plants. Violets and geraniums bloomed gaily, as if unaware of the sorry surroundings.

"Pretty, ain't they?"

Arleen turned her attention to the center of the room and the big brass bed. A tiny, birdlike woman, with bright blue eyes belying her age, and curly gray hair softening her face, was propped up in the middle of the bed, covered by a patchwork quilt.

"Very pretty," Arleen said softly. "You must have a green thumb."

The woman shook her head, and twisted around to look at the man in the soiled undershirt. "Not me, miss. It's my husband, Al, who has the green thumb. My, but you should have seen the flowers he grew when we had a downstairs place over on Kirby Street. There was windows all around the kitchen," she said, a wistful note coming into her voice. "Boxes and boxes of flowers Al planted all around them windows. Folks used to stop just to look at them, they looked that pretty.

"We're kind of down on our luck right now—" with an apologetic glance around the room—"but one of these days we're gonna have a nice place again, and maybe even a yard where Al can grow all kinds of flowers." She gave her husband an affectionate smile.

Arleen watched Al Ryan's lips tighten. He said harshly, "Don't go giving the new nurse a pack of lies, Neelie! You know we're not going to get out of this place, unless it's to move to someplace worse!" He glared at Arleen. "In thirty years of marriage I never did provide Neelie with a really decent living, and I'm providing her with less than that now. The welfare's taking care of her, not me!"

"Now, Al, honey," the woman chided him. "You don't want to talk like that. Why, it's been a real good life we've had, Al, and I wouldn't have missed having it with you for anything. Things'll get better. You just wait and see if they won't. And I'm not going to be always laying in bed like this, either. You just mind that's the truth!"

Al Ryan shot his wife a baffled, angry glance. He shook his head, and his hair, white and thick, stood cloudlike on top of his head.

"Listen to her!" he appealed helplessly to Arleen. "I'm sixty years old. Nobody's going to hire me. I'm too old to get a job, and too young for social security. I keep telling her, but she won't listen! Sometimes I honestly think she even believes that stuff she says, about how everything's going to get real good for us one of these days!" His Adam's apple worked vigorously as he talked. "You make her see," he told Arleen, "that she's got to face up to what's real. If she don't, she's going to end up in one of them psycho wards. You make her see that!"

Neelie Ryan smiled sweetly up at Arleen. "Now, ain't that just like a man? Always getting depressed, like they don't know the bright side's there, if you just look hard enough for it?"

She squinted up at Arleen. "My, but you don't hardly look old enough to be a nurse."

Arleen laughed and took off her cape, putting it carefully on the foot of the bed. "Thanks," she said, "but I'm twenty-three."

"My," Neelie Ryan said, "twenty-three. Imagine that." Her faded blue eyes held a faraway, dreamy look. "I can remember when I was twenty-three. I was doing housework and taking care of three kids for a widower upstate. I always liked doing that kind of work. It's a whole lot better than working in some dime store. I felt that, in a way, I was helping people who needed help." She smiled, a sudden, secret smile. "But then Al come along and I forgot all about wanting to help people. I couldn't see no one but Al."

The door slammed, and she sighed and said softly, "Poor Al, he feels terrible about not having a job. But it's not as if he don't try. He's the tryingest man. Even that Mrs. Gibbons from welfare has to admit that, even if she don't like Al." She sighed again. "Al's so proud." As if that were an explanation.

Arleen asked for hot water, and Neelie Ryan shook her head regretfully. "These are cold-water flats. We have to

8

heat water. There's a pan under the stove. I'm sorry Al went off like he did, he could have heated the water for you. Watch out for that gas burner. It's a kind of temperamental."

"I'll make out fine," Arleen told her. "I'm used to temperamental gas burners. We have one in the apartment where I live."

Neelie Ryan laughed. "You're real pretty, too," she said, admiringly. "What happened to the other nurse, Mrs. Kitchener? She was a very nice lady."

Arleen set out alcohol and cotton, soap, washcloth and a large, absorbent towel. She had been told to include towels, washcloths and soap in her supply bag, because most of the people with whom she would deal would deal would not consider such articles as real necessities.

"She decided to have a baby," Arleen said, in answer to the woman's question.

"My, that's nice," Neelie said. "I'm real glad for her."

Arleen used a gentle touch in sponging the thin, small body. "Now, I'm going to give you an alcohol rub, Mrs. Ryan," she said cheerfully.

"My but that feels good," she said, as Arleen skillfully massaged her shoulders and back. "Sometimes the other nurse wouldn't have time to give me a massage, but when she did have the time, oh, but it sure felt so good. You don't want to call me Mrs. Ryan, miss. I'm Neelie. Everybody calls me Neelie. Even kids."

Finished with the rub, Arleen got out a big box of dusting powder and patted Neelie's neck, back and shoulders generously with it. She got a comb and combed her soft gray hair into becoming order.

"There now," she said cheerfully, putting the things back into her satchel, "you look all pert and pretty."

Neelie nodded happily. "I smell like a flower garden, too." she said. Wistfully she added, "I like pretty things, pretty smells, pretty flowers, pretty dresses."

Pity tugged at Arleen's heart. Impulsively she leaned over and patted the older woman's hand. "See you day after tomorrow," she told her.

She frowned. She didn't like leaving Neelie alone, and her husband had not yet returned. "Is there anyone in the building I could get to stay with you until your husband comes back?"

Neelie smiled confidently. "Don't you worry none about me. I won't be alone very long—my Al never stays away long. He worries about me." She said it proudly, with the air of a woman who knows she's cared about.

"Don't you get the wrong impression about Al," she told Arleen anxiously. "He's a good man. It's just. . . ." the thin, small hands moved on the patchwork quilt, folding and creasing it along the edge. "Well, Al's one of those people who just don't have good luck, no matter how much they work." Earnestly, "But you know what I believe? I believe that everybody's got one big chunk of luck that belongs just to them. And me and Al's going to get our chunk before we die."

That stab of pity 'hit Arleen again. She thought fiercely, "I must not allow myself to identify with my patients! Have I forgotten already what Mrs. Hitzer drummed into my head in third-year training?"

A nurse must not identify with her patients, because if she allows this, the personal element enters in and some of her efficiency is destroyed.

Arleen bent to smooth the quilt across Neelie's chest. "That's a beautiful quilt," she said. "I've been admiring it."

Neelie said proudly, "I made it myself, and by hand. Every last stitch of it."

In the hall, Arleen nearly collided with a tall, thin young man hurrying toward the stairs that led to the last floor of the building.

She was aware of gray eyes sweeping over her face as if she were not there; dark hair badly in need of a trim. He hurried by her with not so much as a "sorry."

Arleen stared after him. She was not used to rudeness in men where she was concerned, nor was she used to being ignored as if she did not exist.

She became aware of Al Ryan plodding up the stairs, a paper-wrapped parcel under one arm. He looked at her, then followed her eyes as she looked toward the upper stairs.

"Who was that?" She couldn't resist the question.

"Him?" Al shifted the parcel from under his arm to his hands. "That's Dr. Wynter. Imagine a doctor living in this neighborhood, taking care of people who can't afford to feed themselves, let alone pay a doctor." He shook his head. "He's as crazy as Neelie, always figuring some miracle's going to come along. Well, before he starves to death, somebody ought to tell him that miracles don't happen to people like us!"

With what Arleen knew was a gesture of defiance, he pulled open the paper bag and revealed its contents. "Know

10

what a wino is, miss? Well, I'll tell you. It's a guy who gets drunk on wine because it's the best he can afford."

Arleen said nothing. Al fingered the cap of the bottle. He said bitterly, "A man's got to have something to get him through the days. You wouldn't know what it's like to ache inside of you like you have a toothache."

Arleen, thinking of Dr. Johnny Thorne, the young intern she had fallen in love with during the last year of nurses' training, thought, "Oh, don't I?"

Johnny had been handsome and cocky, terribly smart, terribly ambitious. When he had asked her to marry him, she had been quite sure that heaven could offer no more.

Five months afterward, almost to the day, he had asked her to return his ring. "I thought it could work," he'd told her. "I know now it couldn't."

Arleen had been unbelieving. "Why wouldn't it work, Johnny? I wasn't going to be only your wife. I was going to be your nurse and your receptionist. I was even going to ... to keep your books." Her voice had broken.

He'd shaken his head impatiently. "You'll make a fine wife for the right man, Arleen. I'm not the right man. I want to climb to the top of my profession, but not by taking one rung of the ladder at a time! I want to leap to the top!"

Arleen had wanted to tell him that she didn't think it was that way in medicine; that you worked your way to the top. But he hadn't given her the chance.

"I've found a gal who can help me make that leap," he'd told her.

"You love her?" Arleen had asked him.

"I want to marry her, if that's what you mean," he'd answered. "She has the money and the influence to help me." At Arleen's shocked look he'd added, "Now, honey, don't look that way. I've never pretended to be a knight in shining armor, have I?"

She'd had to admit that he hadn't; that he'd never pretended to be anything except what he was. The dreams had been on her side alone. And the love.

Johnny's love was the surface kind, never going deep enough to bruise. She had made her mind up, after Johnny, that never again would she let herself be hurt.

She liked men; she enjoyed their company. But she determined that never again would she allow herself to fall in love.

It was over a year since she had made that promise, and

11

her heart was still safe inside the invincible, love-resistant shield she had built to protect it.

Sighing, Arleen glanced down at her notebook. One more call to make in the building. "Mrs. Mario Luigui. Eight months pregnant. Missed last two check-ups at clinic."

The Luigui apartment was on the floor below. Thinking that it was easier walking downstairs than up, Arleen headed for the stairs.

CHAPTER 2

THE LUIGUI apartment was in startling contrast to the Ryan place, where at least an attempt was made to keep it neat, and the window plants had provided brightness and color.

Here there was appalling squalor. Arleen had difficulty repressing her dismay at the filth and ugliness of the three rooms into which were crowded, as a quick glance at her notebook told her, ten human beings.

Anna Luigui was half lying, half sitting on a cot against one wall. Her coarse red face looked puffy and bloated. Incredibly dirty feet stretched out from beneath an equally dirty skirt.

Arleen turned her attention to the thin, undersized boy who had let her into the apartment. His nose was running and there was a patch of scaly skin on one side of his face that looked like ringworm. But it was impossible to tell, under all the dirt.

She started to hand him a tissue from her purse, but the moment she bent toward him he pulled back wildly, dashed to the far side of the room, and huddled against a wall.

A young girl of perhaps fifteen or sixteen, in a sweater a good two sizes too small, and a skirt that hugged her slender body as if she had been poured into it, laughed. "Poor Pietro. He's so used to getting banged he thought that was what you were going to do."

Arleen turned her gaze on the girl. She was quite pretty, or would be if she would wash off some of the heavy make-up she wore.

She returned Arleen's look with mockery.

Arleen shook her head. "I'm sorry your little brother got

that impression. I only wanted him to let me look at that patch on his cheek."

The woman on the cot laid down the comic book she'd been reading. She put a finger to the side of her head and tapped. "Pietro ain't right in the head," she said. "That's what makes him act like that."

The girl swirled around to glare at the woman. "Pietro isn't any more crazy than you are!" She flung at her. "If you'd stop banging him around the head every time he comes near you, he wouldn't be so scared of people!"

The woman glared back. "Two years you go to high school, and you think you're so smart! You make me sick. And them bad boys you run around with. Don't think I don't know about them? You want to get put in jail, huh? Answer me that. Huh? Girls who think they're so smart, that's what happens to them. Ain't that right?" She turned her attention to Arleen.

Arleen ignored the attempt to bring her into the argument. "I'm the visiting nurse, Mrs. Luigui. You *are* Mrs. Luigui?" The woman nodded sullenly. "You didn't show up for your last two appointments at the clinic," Arleen said, speaking slowly and firmly. "These check-ups are for your own protection, and for that of your unborn baby."

The woman shrugged and spat out the words. "Eight kids. That's enough. Huh, that's enough? Them doctors at that clinic, they're always saying, 'Now, Mrs. Luigui, you got to be careful you don't lose your baby. You got to be careful!'" Her laughter rasped. "And why I got to be so careful? Huh? One less kid and the others don't have to shove over in bed to make room for another one. Huh, how do you like that?"

Arleen wet her lips as she stared at Mrs. Luigui. It wasn't possible for a woman to feel that way. It wasn't possible! The way she talked it sounded as if she didn't care if something happened to her baby. No, it wasn't even that. She talked as if she *wanted* something to happen to it!

Arleen felt a tug at her skirt. A small grimy hand was gripping a fold of the blue cloth. Wide, dark eyes in a small, dirty face gazed upward. "Pretty," the child lisped. "Pretty lady."

Arleen felt her heart jerk as she stared down at the child. Mrs. Luigui hadn't meant what she'd said. She was a victim of prenatal blues. It happened in young wives afraid they appeared ugly in their husband's eyes. And in women like Mrs. Luigui, who had quite a few children and were exhausted by the endless demands made upon them. Of course she had not meant what she'd said.

13

The child's wide, wistful eyes touched Arleen's heart. She wondered if she still had the candy bar she'd bought last night. She could not remember having eaten it.

She opened her purse, being very careful to make no sudden movement that would frighten this child, as she had frightened the little boy when she'd first come in.

He still leaned against the wall, solemnly watching her and the little girl, one grimy thumb stuck between his pale lips.

Arleen found the candy bar and handed it to the little girl clinging to her skirts. The child grabbed the candy, her small hand closing around it fiercely. She turned from Arleen, letting go of her skirt, and it was suddenly as if Arleen had set off an explosion.

The child clutching the candy bar was surrounded by screaming, clawing children who bit and kicked and grabbed to get the candy for their own.

Arleen was shocked into silence for a moment. Then she said to the woman on the bed and the girl lounging against the rickety table, "Make them stop! Don't let them fight like that!"

The woman shrugged heavy shoulders. "Oh, don't mind them; they always fight. They'll stop after while."

Arleen looked helplessly toward the girl. There was bitter mockery on the young lips as she stared back at Arleen. "What's wrong? Haven't you ever seen kids fight over something they want? How much candy do you think they get? Of course they'd fight over who was going to get it. You should have known that!"

Arleen said unhappily, "I didn't realize. . . ."

The dark head cocked to one side. "No, I guess you wouldn't. I guess *you* never had to fight over a piece of candy. I guess *you* had all the candy you wanted." The dark eyes slid over Arleen in envious scorn. "All of *everything!*"

Guilt stabbed Arleen and she could no longer look at this bitter child. It was true. Her parents had provided her with all of the necessities and a lot of the luxuries. There'd always been enough money. She had never known what it was to be without money.

The guilt stabbed harder. "It's not my fault," she told herself. "I'm not to blame!" Nevertheless she felt the need to make amends because she'd never known what it was to have to fight over a bar of candy.

There was the five dollars in her purse she'd been saving to put down as a deposit on that green dress she so liked in

14

Arden's window. She didn't need the dress, and five dollars would provide the Luigui children with a generous supply of treats.

Impulsively she got out the five-dollar bill and handed it to Anna Luigui. The woman's head jerked up. She looked at Arleen with real interest for the first time since she had come into the apartment.

Arleen said, looking at the mother, but in reality speaking to the girl by the table, "Use it to buy some treat for the children." With sudden firmness she added, "It will also give you bus fare to the clinic."

Anna Luigui was turning the bill over and over in her hand. Her head jerked up when Arleen spoke. "Yeah, I be there." Suddenly there was a shining ring to her voice. "Maybe I do better with things if I had a better daughter. But that Rose—" shooting an angry glance at the girl by the table— "she don't lift one finger to help. Not one finger. All she thinks about is telling me how much smarter she is than I am. And dolling herself up so boys will look at her!"

Arleen said firmly, "Be at the clinic at two on Wednesday, Mrs. Luigui." She directed a hesitant smile around the room, but the children didn't smile back; they stood in little huddles, regarding her mutely.

Arleen let herself out. As she stood ready to turn the doorknob, she looked back into the room and saw that Rose Luigui was regarding her, the dark eyes made even darker by anger.

Arleen stepped out into the hall, closing the door quietly behind her. "I should have realized," she thought, "that one candy bar wouldn't near go around for that many children."

The five dollars, she knew, was not going to make up for what she had not known. And to Rose Luigui's way of thinking, Arleen realized that what she had not known was the ugliness of Rose's kind of poverty.

She was surprised to find the young doctor who had bumped into her earlier waiting in the lower hall.

"I have the time to apologize for bumping into you," he said. "I do apologize." He had a most engaging grin, Arleen thought.

"I have a patient on the top floor," he explained. "Usually she sends for me once a week, saying she's dying. She has a bad heart, so I can't be certain that she isn't."

"He not only has a very nice smile," Arleen found herself thinking, "he also has the nicest eyes. I like that shade of gray."

15

"I was rushing up to see her when I bumped into you," he went on. The light brows drew slightly together. "You looked upset just now."

"Upset?" Arleen gave a rueful laugh. "I just left the Luigui apartment. How can people. . . ."

He cut in, his voice gentle, "Live like that? People live in all sorts of ways. They bring up defenses to allow themselves to live that way. You'll have to get used to people like the Luiguis." His eyes scanned the uniform. "A visiting nurse has to accustom herself to the kind of special ugliness that lives here alongside the people." Abruptly he added, "I'm Dr. Mark Wynter. Now that I've introduced myself, why not tell me your name, and then I think we should be properly introduced."

Arleen laughed. "Arleen Anderson."

He slanted a grin at her. "Called Arleen for short, I presume?" He stopped laughing, and in repose Arleen thought his face looked very sad. "Now, Miss Arleen Anderson, could I buy you a cup of coffee at Barney's? It's a very unclassy place, but he makes fairly good coffee, and he's fairly clean. I must warn you, only fairly clean."

"I could use a cup of coffee," Arleen told him. She hesitated. "But I'll accept your offer only if you'll let it be dutch."

He shook his head. "I see you've already heard about my poverty. But I assure you I can afford to buy two cups of coffee. I'm a special customer of Barney's. He never charges me more than five cents a cup."

Seeming to take her consent for granted, he stepped ahead of her, opening the door, holding it until she stepped out onto the cracked and littered sidewalk. A vagrant April breeze seized bits of paper from the gutter and sent them sailing gaily through the air like miniature kites.

Arleen looked at her car, and let out a gasp. Garbage had been flung at her windshield, and bits of orange and tomato littered the hood.

Behind her, Mark Wynter heard her gasp, stopped for a second to survey the car, said quickly, "Wait here. I won't be but a moment," and disappeared with long-legged strides down the street and around a corner.

When he reappeared he had three small boys in tow. He marched them up to the car and said sternly, "Miss Anderson is a friend of mine. I don't like you playing such tricks on friends of mine. I want you to have her car cleaned by the time we get back. Understand?"

16

Still frowning fiercely, he let go of the boys, dug a hand into a pocket and came up with some change, which he distributed evenly among the three. "That's for candy for each of you. But first the car has to be cleaned."

As she and Mark walked away, Arleen asked curiously, "Will they do what you told them to?"

Mark gave a wry grin. "It's a gamble," he told her. "I don't always win."

CHAPTER 3

MAY IN SALTBORO differed from April only in that it was hotter and drier. Litter from the city streets, swept by the occasional gusts of fierce wind, choked the nostrils and the throat with dust. The factories belched smoke and grime into the air until it seemed to rest like a heavy load across Arleen's chest.

As her eyes stung and her throat ached from the smog-laden air, she would think, with a pang of homesickness, of the fresh green lawns and the clean air, scented with fresh-cut clover, that characterized her home.

Not the tiny apartment she shared with Evelyn Drew, a nurse at Saltboro's General Hospital. The place was hot and uncomfortable, in spite of the window fan she and Evelyn had installed. Home to Arleen was still the big, airy, clean rooms in the house at the end of Main Street, back in Carson.

As Arleen drove the small black coupé into the ·Leland Street area this Wednesday morning in late May, she seemed more aware than ever before of the bleak ugliness of the place; the air of hopeless defeat and dismal unconcern that crowded the lungs like the choking smog.

She parked her car and walked toward the tenement building that was her destination this morning.· She no longer feared to leave her car unlocked. Mark Wynter seemed to have an uncanny control over the children of the area. Since that first morning, when Mark had collared the young culprits, her car and possessions had been left strictly alone.

Evelyn, her roommate, tall and blonde, filled with the joy and excitement of being young, was wont to tease Arleen about Dr. Wynter.

"Aha, the knight in shining armor! Did he come on a white horse and swoop you up in his arms?"

She enjoyed Arleen's blushing. "It isn't a matter of modesty at all," she'd tell her. "It's a matter of pigmentation." Her blue eyes would twinkle at Arleen's increasing discomfiture.

Lately she had waxed serious on the subject of Mark Wynter. "Any girl is a complete fool if she lets herself become involved with a dedicated man, and Mark Wynter is the most dedicated man I've ever known. You fall in love with a man like that, and it'll be just as if you had cut your own throat."

Arleen would shrug if off. "Just because I have a few cups of coffee with Dr. Wynter, you've got me involved with him. For your information, Evelyn, I'm not going to get involved emotionally with any man. So stop worrying about me. I'm perfectly capable of taking care of myself."

Evelyn still was not convinced. "Methinks the lady doth protest too much," she said. "You're the stars-and-moonlight kind. They always fall hard. And Dr. Wynter is not, and I don't think ever will be, husband material. Sometimes I wonder (and I'm not the only one, I can tell you) if Mark Wynter even knows women exist . . . as women."

Arleen said quietly, "I was in love once. I'm not making that mistake again."

Evelyn hooted. "Once? Honey, I've been in love a dozen times. When I stop falling in love, I'll be old. But you, honey, you're different. You take it seriously."

Arleen's heels clicked on the pavement as she walked with her usual briskness. "Yes," she thought, "I do take love seriously. That's why I'm never going to fall in love again."

Once you've walked too close to a fire and got burned, there is no desire in you to walk so close again, Arleen thought grimly.

Even at this hour of the morning the sun beat down mercilessly. Arleen thought of the staggering heat that must already be filling Neelie Ryan's top-floor room, and made almost unlivable the three dark, narrow rooms of the Luigui menage.

Anna Luigui's baby had arrived seven days before, a darkeyed, beautiful little girl with an incredible amount of soft, black hair.

She had arrived healthy and whole, in spite of the fact that Anna Luigui had not returned to the clinic after all. "Who

18

wants a live baby?" she'd said sullenly. "A dead one will suit me just fine."

Arleen sighed. Anna must love her baby by now. Who would not love such a beautiful little girl? Anna and the baby had been home from the hospital for four days. Charity patients were kept there only the bare minimum of three days, unless there were complications.

It seemed a pity to Arleen that such a tiny baby should have to endure such heat, and . . . yes, neglect. Still, the smaller Luigui children seemed quite attached to the infant.

Yesterday, when she'd gone to bathe the baby, the little girl to whom she'd given the candy bar that first day (she shuddered, the candy-bar episode being something she hated to remember) had come shyly to the door to meet her.

"Our baby's name is Carmella, Miss Anderson," she'd told Arleen, the dark eyes shining in the small, dirty face.

Arleen had smiled at her. "That's a pretty name for a very pretty baby."

Rose Luigui, tight skirt pulled above her knees as she slumped in a chair, said mockingly, "Ma got it from a comic book. Carmella was some super dame."

Her mother's voice screamed at her, "You lie. Always you lie about me. That was your grandmother's name. Oh, my poor mama, it would kill her if she saw how her little Anna has to live." Her voice grated. "And with such a bad daughter!"

"Ha!" Rose said, her voice even more mocking.

Anna Luigui began to cry, whiningly, tears rolling down her fat cheeks, making rivulets in the layers of rouge and dirt that caked her face.

She had thus far successfully fought off all of Arleen's attempts to wash her face. "When I want my face washed, I can do it myself," she'd tell Arleen fiercely. "You ain't paid to come here and bully me, and I ain't letting you do it. I know my rights!"

"You see what a bad daughter I got?" she'd hurled at Arleen. "You see?" She'd glared at Rose. "You get paid back one of these days for how mean you are to your mama. You get paid back!"

Rose had shrugged her way out of the chair. "You make me sick, old lady!" she'd flung viciously at Anna.

Now Arleen pushed open the door of the tenement building. "I think I'll take care of Neelie first," she thought. "My morale needs lifting before I tackle the Luiguis. And Neelie's always so cheerful, although I don't see how she can manage it."

19

Arleen had a genuine liking for Neelie Ryan. She admired her courage and her determined cheerfulness in spite of all the odds against her.

She plodded up the hot, stuffy stairs to the even hotter, stuffier, upper-floor apartments. She carried with her a sack of candy for the Luigui children.

She knew candy wasn't the answer; that the children needed eggs and meat and vegetables and milk. Lots of good, rich milk. She'd broached the subject to the welfare visitor and had come up against fierce antagonism.

"Would you prefer steak or chops for our welfare clients, Miss Anderson? Strawberries out of season? Perhaps caviar and avocado might appeal to their taste. Air-conditioning, perhaps? It gets quite unbearably hot in Saltboro in June and July."

Arleen had flushed. "Miss Gibbons, I wasn't meaning. . . ."

Her answer had been a cold, crisp, "You do your job, Miss Anderson, and let us at the Welfare Department take care of our own. We do the best we can on the funds we're allotted."

Arleen grimaced. The candy provided the children with a treat, at least. If it wasn't enough, at least it was something.

She had never made the mistake of handing Anna Luigui any money, after that first time. She had discovered to her dismay that Anna had taken the money and used it for liquor rather than for the children.

Arleen had been amazed that a woman eight months pregnant could be in any condition to get drunk.

Rose Luigui, dark eyes mocking as always, had told her scornfully, "Ma's always in condition to get drunk, if she's got the money. And you gave her that!"

Al Ryan had the window open, but it did nothing to cool the stifling room. Neelie was propped up in bed, looking wan and tired, but her eyes turned toward Arleen when she walked into the room, and the old aliveness still showed in them.

"Why, it's Miss Anderson. Al, it's Miss Anderson come to do for me."

Al, slumped in a rocking chair by the breezeless window, turned listless, bloodshot eyes toward Arleen. It was evident that he'd been drinking heavily. The sour-sweet odor of cheap wine filled the room.

Neelie didn't let on. She said, affection in her voice, "Al's

20

been sponging my face and arms with cold water all morning. I tell you, it sure has felt good."

Al got to his feet, swaying slightly. His eyes were angry, but behind the anger Arleen thought he looked ready to cry.

"Why don't you tell her I made a few pennies and used them to get myself drunk with, instead of getting you some little thing you might like?" he roared at her.

Neelie said gently, her voice directed at Arleen, but her eyes on her husband, "Al had kind of a rough time this morning. He got up real early and walked clear over to this place on Tenth, thinking they were hiring, but they weren't. He walked all the way back, too."

There was savagery in Al Ryan's voice. "They wasn't hiring *older* men!" he said. "I'm too old to live, and I can't die! I'm no good to anybody, not even myself. I ought to hang myself. That's a cheap way to die!"

Neelie said quietly, "You're all I've got, Al. I don't know what I'd do without you."

He stared at her for a second, his lips quivering, then turned and slammed out of the room.

"I know Al drinks," Neelie said slowly, "but he can't help himself. He's one of those people who, when they can't see no way out of something, has just got to do something to try and make the awful feeling in them go away." Her quiet gaze met Arleen's. "My Al's a good man," she said. "And he'd never do something that would leave me alone. Al would never do a thing like that."

Outside, on the fire escape, a bedraggled sparrow lit for a second and then flew off. Neelie's eyes followed the bird. "Oh, my," she said, "know what I'd like? I guess it'll sound silly to you, but I'd sure like to see that place in California the swallows come back to every year. Capistrano, I guess they call it. Wouldn't it be something to be there and see all them birds come back every year to that same place?"

Arleen, bathing the thin arms and shoulders, nodded. "Tourists come from all over just to see it." Impulsively she added, "Maybe you'll get to see Capistrano, Neelie. It could happen."

Neelie nodded happily. "Sure, why not? There's no law against it, is there? There's no law saying a person can't hope. That's what I keep telling Al."

Arleen's upper lip and forehead were beaded with moisture, and breathing was like pulling furnace air into her lungs.

If it was this hot in May, what was it going to be like in June and July?

Neelie Ryan, as if understanding Arleen's thoughts, said, "It's unseasonably hot for this time of year. It don't get no hotter than this in full summer." She smiled at Arleen, as if she were the one to be comforted. "A body gets used to things," she said. "I expect the good Lord knows some things has got to be gotten used to, so He lets you get used to 'em."

Arleen said, with sudden bitterness, "You should have a fan in here. At least it would stir up the air a little. Anything would help."

She massaged Neelie's shoulders and the back of her neck. "My," the woman said appreciatively, "that makes me feel a heap better."

Arleen sponged her face again with cool water. It wasn't sensible to put on powder, because she knew that within seconds Neelie would begin to perspire again.

As she put her things away into her bag, she said, "Know what, Neelie? I'm going to bring you a fan the next time I come. And if there's any breeze blowing at all, you'll get some of it."

Neelie looked doubtful. "Oh, I don't think you should go to all that fuss, Miss Anderson. I don't think the landlord would like me to use that extra electricity."

Arleen said fiercely, "I don't care what he likes, Neelie! I'll say I prescribed it for you. And if that doesn't take care of it, I'll pay for the extra electricity myself!"

She bent over Neelie, squeezing the woman's hand in her strong, young grip.

Neelie smiled up at her. "You're a fine girl," she said. "A real fine girl, Miss Anderson."

Arleen met Al Ryan in the hall. He flashed her an angry glance, but did not speak.

Arleen walked down to the second-floor landing. She thought, "I'm not a fine girl. It's only that I feel guilty because I have that big window fan in my apartment, and if it gets too hot I can go out to an air-conditioned movie or a restaurant. Neelie can't do that. And I can't rest in my own comfort unless I try and do something for her!"

As she neared the Luigui apartment, she could hear the unhappy sound of a baby crying.

22

CHAPTER 4

As ALWAYS, the dirt, litter and abject misery of the Luigui apartment hit Arleen like a blow across the face.

She found Anna Luigui lying down, clad in a not too clean nightgown, her bare, dirty feet trailing over the side of the cot.

At the table, Rose Luigui was spreading peanut butter on bread for the Luigui children crowded around her. The youngest member of the Luigui clan reposed on a pillow on the table, beside the peanut butter jar. She was crying in fierce, heartbreaking wails.

Rose, unaware of anyone else in the room but the waiting, clutching children and the crying baby, said, an edge of hysteria in her voice, "Shut up! Shut up, will you? If you keep up that yelling I'll . . . I'll brain you!"

And then, as Arleen watched, she let the knife drop into the peanut butter jar while she reached down with fierce tenderness and picked up Carmella.

"I didn't mean that. Rose didn't mean that. . . ." Suddenly, feeling the strange presence in the room, she lifted her head and stared, flushed and sullen-eyed, at Arleen.

"What do you think you're looking at?" she flung at her, as she let the baby drop back gently onto the pillow, making no further effort to quiet its cries.

She retrieved the knife and once again began spreading peanut butter on the bread, to the accompanying unmelodic wails of Carmella.

"Welcome to breakfast, Miss Anderson," she told Arleen, in the familiar mocking voice. "Besides the peanut butter sandwiches the menu always has powdered milk to drink. Oh, it's warm and it's gaggy to taste, but it's very good for you. Ask Miss Gibbons! She drinks it herself . . . to hear her tell it!"

Arleen walked over and picked up Carmella. "Perhaps she'll stop crying if she's held," she said.

She was surprised to find that the baby was not only dry, but bathed and clean. Arleen felt quite certain Anna had had nothing to do with it.

She looked at Rose. "Has the baby had her formula?"

23

Rose nodded, without looking up. "Next one's due at twelve o'clock." She finished with the sandwiches and began pouring the powdered skim milk into an assorted array of cracked glasses and handleless cups.

Arleen said awkwardly, "I brought the children a little treat of candy. You can hand it out to them."

Rose said, in a hard voice, "Hand it out yourself, nurse lady. You're the one who brought it."

Arleen flushed. She waited until the children had finished the milk, and then she carefully divided the candy among them. Their greedy, clutching hunger still appalled her.

Rose pushed the glasses and dirty cutlery to one side, not bothering to wash them. "We're going to use them again," she told Arleen lightly. "Why bother washing them?"

She watched the younger children devouring the candy. She'd scorned any for herself. "That's your lunch, kids," she told them. "After a big treat like that, who needs lunch?"

Arleen didn't dare look at the girl, or speak, knowing that if she did, the anger would show not only in her face but in her voice.

She had never come up against such open antagonism in her life before. Ignoring Rose, she found a basin, filled it with cold water, and sponged off Carmella. The infant stopped its restless crying and was asleep in Arleen's arms as she finished drying her.

She tried to find a cool place in the room in which to put the baby, but there was no cool spot in the entire apartment.

When she straightened from putting the infant in her basket, she wiped at the perspiration gathering on her forehead. She caught Rose's eye. "What you need here," Arleen said, "is a fan."

The young girl's arched brows went up a shade higher. "Oh?" she said. "Is it uncomfortable for you, nurse? I'm so sorry, but our air conditioner is out of order. The butler's having it fixed. Maybe next time you come. . . ."

Arleen said levelly, "Rose, do you think hating me is going to change things?"

Rose shrugged, and said airily, "It keeps me occupied."

Anna Luigui, engrossed in reading one of her inevitable comic books, had barely glanced up when Arleen entered the room. The baby's crying had not seemed to affect her at all.

"Mrs. Luigui. . . ." Arleen moved toward her purposefully, but suddenly Pietro strained himself into her view.

She frowned, and glanced at Rose. "That eruption on his skin could be ringworm or impetigo. It should be washed and looked at. Do you suppose he would let me near enough to him to take a look?"

Rose shrugged. "Search me. Pietro just don't like people, especially women." She gave a bitter glance at her mother. "Not that he hasn't got reasons!"

Anna heard. She lifted her head and said sullenly, "Don't go talking about your mama. I try to keep you decent. You just tell the nurse what time you come in this morning! Huh? Four o'clock in the morning she come in. What kind of time is that for a decent girl to come home, huh? Where she was? She don't tell me. Ain't none of my business, she tells me! Her own mama! None of my business!"

Arleen tried to sidestep the argument. She said sternly, "I'm sure Pietro wouldn't be afraid, Rose, if you'd tell him that all I want to do is to wash his face and look at the breaking out on his skin."

Rose merely shrugged, and Arleen said coldly, "Both impetigo and ringworm are contagious. If Pietro does have either of those, he could give it to the entire family."

Rose said carefully, "Is dirt contagious, too, nurse lady? I know the answer to that one. It sure is." She pointed to Anna's feet hanging over the side of the cot. "Ma's given her dirt to everybody else in the family. You got something to cure dirt, nurse lady? If you ain't, you might just as well quit talking!"

Anna howled in indignation. "Listen to her. Listen to her! And me having to lay here and take that kind of talk from her. Too sick to get up on my feet and go at her!"

Arleen said quietly, "You don't have to stay in bed, Mrs. Luigui. In fact, the doctor wants you up on your feet, doing your usual work. Women recover their strength much faster that way."

Anna frowned and said belligerently, "That doctor ever have a baby? You ever have a baby? Well, then, don't you go telling me what it's like!" She moved her big bulk on the narrow cot.

Arleen said, "Would you like me to give you a sponge bath? You'll feel much better."

Anna shook her head. "I want a bath, I'll take one myself!"

Arlene sighed. You tried and you tried, and you got exactly nowhere. She closed her bag. "I'll weigh Carmella next time I come. It would be a shame to disturb her when she's asleep. Is she taking her formula all right?"

Anna shrugged. "Ask Rose. I been too sick to pay attention to that squalling kid. Rose does what's got to be done . . . when she ain't out running in the streets all night!"

Arleen turned to look, but Rose had vanished. She let her gaze wander to the Luigui children, sprawled about the room in various stages of undress.

She knew there was a Mr. Luigui, but evidently he kept his distance whenever Arleen showed up. She said, "Is your husband working, Mrs. Luigui?"

It was the wrong question, Arleen knew, the moment she'd asked it. Mrs. Luigui's broad face reddened and the small eyes, in their layers of fat, narrowed.

"You come here spying for Welfare?" she said. "That it?"

Arleen shook her head. She said calmly, "Of course not. I have nothing whatever to do with Welfare. I was just wondering about your husband."

Anna said sullenly, "My Tony works when he gets work. He don't get work. Whata you think of that?"

Arleen was glad to escape Anna's sullen viciousness, and the smell of the tiny apartment, composed of heat and dirt and too many unwashed bodies.

Outside, she stood for a moment on the cracked sidewalk in front of the building. She closed her eyes briefly, having no wish to paint the picture of the street in her mind. It was already much too vivid, so that sometimes when she awoke at night she could see it.

Across the street, lounging in front of a poolhall with a torn awning, were three boys. In spite of the heat they each wore identical black leather jackets with a rooster garishly painted on the back.

Feeling their gaze on her, Arleen deliberately directed a blank, impersonal stare in their direction. One of them, a short, thin boy with his blond hair arranged in an extravagant way, gave back her stare from heavy-lidded, mean eyes. Turning to his companions, he gave a high, shrill laugh.

A tremor of fear found its way along Arleen's spine. In the nearly seven weeks she had worked as visiting nurse in the area, she had had no sign of trouble. It was said that nurses and doctors could travel more or less freely in most of the trouble spots.

Still. . . . Arleen wet her lips and determined not to show fear. She walked with quick, resolute steps toward her car.

Out of the corner of an eye, she watched one of the boys

26

detach himself from the other two, flip a cigarette butt with utmost contempt toward the gutter, hook his thumbs in the belt of his low-slung jeans and saunter across the street toward Arleen. Behind him there were loud snickers of laughter.

It required valiant effort for Arleen, almost at the car, to force herself to look at the boy crossing the street. But she did it.

He was taller than the others, and although he was thin, Arleen could sense the wiry strength that was in him. Dark, curly hair gave him a boyish look which his mocking, scornful eyes and bitter mouth belied.

Her fingers touched the door handle. She opened it, and forced herself to climb without haste behind the wheel. Equally without haste, as if she were not aware of the boy walking toward her, Arleen turned the key in the switch.

She thought, "How in the world can I act unafraid, when I'm scared to death?"

The dark-haired boy's voice was a drawl of harshness. "You going somewhere, lady?"

Arleen made herself look up at him. He was perhaps eighteen . . . nineteen. It was hard to tell, she thought. He was one of the old-young. She'd seen far too many of them in the seven weeks she'd worked in the Leland Street slum area.

"Yes," she said, "I'm going back to the county health department; I work out of there. Then this afternoon I'm going to make more calls on sick and convalescent people who can't afford a regular nurse."

She was surprised to find how steady and calm her voice came out.

The boy looked undecided. He frowned, scrubbed the toe of his shoe against the side of the curb and said harshly, "They shouldn't send women around places like this by themselves."

Arleen said quietly, "I'm a nurse. Nurses have to go where they're needed."

The boy scowled at her, kicked at the gutter, then turned away. "You'd better get out of here," he flung at her over his shoulder. "Get that heap of yours going and get out of here!"

The switch key was on, but the motor hadn't started. Arleen's foot trembled as she pressed it down on the starter. The motor began purring smoothly. Across the street, Arleen decided an argument was going on, and she had the uncomfortable feeling that she was the cause of it.

She shifted into low and was ready to take off when Mark Wynter's low, pleasant voice greeted her.

"You're gunning the motor, Miss Anderson—Arleen for short—and that's no way to drive. Hasn't anyone ever told you the facts about cars?"

Arleen thought she had never in her whole life heard anything more wonderful than the sound of Mark Wynter's voice at that particular moment.

She turned to look at him, and the trembling she'd kept from her voice until now was evident as she asked, "Do you always show up at the right moment?"

His gray eyes scanned her face. "I try," he said.

Although he did not turn his head, Arleen knew that he was aware of the three across the street. "Trouble?" he asked, his voice quiet.

Arleen still felt shaky. She said, her voice unsteady, "I was afraid there was going to be. This . . . this dark-haired boy came over to the car, but all he did was to tell me I shouldn't be around here by myself, and I should take my car and get away from here. I don't think the others liked his just walking away from me like that."

Mark said slowly, "Probably not. But they'll listen to him. Peter—that's the boy—Peter Rossi is the leader of the Roosters, and so long as he's their leader, they'll do what he says."

His voice softened. "The Roosters aren't women attackers," he said. "Probably what they had in mind was a little excitement for a hot, dull day. If Peter had got you scared —riled up—crying—why, it would have given them a couple of laughs."

Arleen stared at him, shocked. "What dreadful minds they must have!"

Mark Wynter shrugged and said slowly, "What dreadful lives they have to live."

Arleen, looking beyond the car, saw Rose Luigui swing out of the doorway of the apartment building and stroll, hips swinging in the tight skirt, across the street toward the poolhall. Immediately there was a chorus of whistles as the boys turned their full attention on her.

Arleen shook her head. "Her mother said Rose didn't come in until four this morning. I don't know if. . . ."

Mark cut in savagely, "It's probably not the first time, and it won't be the last. Rose is intelligent. She's got it in

28

her to make something of herself, if she had the chance. But she won't get the chance, and she'll go down and down."

He straightened his shoulders; sighed. "Peter Rossi is intelligent, too," he said. "He wanted to go to high school, but he couldn't make it. Now he doesn't care—about anything or anybody. His father is a drunkard. When Peter was small he'd beat him until he was senseless. He's afraid to beat Peter now, and he doesn't beat Peter's mother if Peter's around. It's left its mark on the boy. He's never been in court yet, but that's only because he's never been caught. Some day he will be, and that'll be the beginning."

He sounded savage and angry and bitter. Arleen said, curiously, "Why didn't he do what the others wanted him to? Why did he just walk away from me? Perhaps, deep inside of him, he doesn't want to do any of these things, Mark."

Mark shrugged. "That's probably very true. But Peter will do them, because he has to show the world that he doesn't care." His eyes were warm on Arleen's face. "Something about you got through to Peter," he told her. He looked away from her quickly, as if there were something in his face he did not want her to see.

There was a lump in Arleen's throat. She said, past it, "Why, Mark? Why do people have to live like this? Poor Neelie Ryan up there in that stifling room, bedridden, with a weak, drunken husband; the Luiguis . . . poor Rose . . . this Peter Rossi?"

Mark Wynter said tightly, "Ah, now, there's a question. If you find the answer, my dear Miss Anderson, please give it to me. I'm curious. A lot of people are curious about the whys and the wherefores of this particular kind of misery."

He opened the car door and told Arleen to slide over. "I don't have my car," he said, "so I'll drive yours. We'll have a cup of coffee at Barney's."

Arleen knew she shouldn't take the time, but she also knew she was going to. She said lightly, "Hot coffee on a day like this?"

He said firmly, "A hot drink is good for you on a hot day."

Arleen laughed. "You're the doctor," she said.

Across the street, Rose Luigui was strutting along, with the three boys following her.

CHAPTER 5

BARNEY'S WAS incredibly hot, in spite of the whirling fan that made a pretense of cooling the place. Barney Bonardio was a balding man, with a wide grin and a paunch. He chewed garlic interminably all day long. He was chewing it now, as Arleen and Mark walked in, and polishing the counter top with a not too clean dish cloth.

He glanced up, greeted them with, "Well, if it ain't the doc and the nurse. It's a shame nobody don't get sick right here in my place." He grinned at Mark. "That ought to tell you, Doc, that it's safe to eat in here; you ain't liable to get ptomaine." He leaned toward Mark, thumped him on the chest with a fat forefinger and laughed again.

"Two coffees," Mark ordered. "And you should do something about that fan. It's using up electricity, and that's all it's doing."

Barney gave the counter a final swish with the cloth. "You ought to do something about the weather, Doc. That fan's doing the best it can with the material on hand." He laughed as if he'd made a good joke.

And then he frowned. "Whatsa matter you don't order nothing but coffee you come here? You think my food ain't good? Why don't you order the lady a hamburger? I got good, fresh meat, just this morning, and for you, Doc, I make it only half price. I don't make a cent on it."

Mark glanced at Arleen. "Hamburger?"

She shook her head. "Not today. It's too hot to eat."

"Next time," Mark said. He directed a mock scowl at Barney. "You chewing garlic again?"

Barney, setting two coffees in thick mugs in front of them, grinned at Mark. "Whatsa matter, Doc, don't them books of yours tell you garlic's good for blood pressure?" He thumped himself fiercely on the chest. "I got fine blood pressure. That's because I eat garlic. Always I eat garlic." He grinned again. "You find something you want to know that ain't in them books of yours, Doc, you come ask old Barney."

Arleen hid a smile. Mark's eyebrows lifted. He said lightly to Barney, "Mind if we take our coffee and sit at that end

30

of the counter, right under the fan? At least we can think we're being cooled off."

Barney waved his hands expansively. "The place is yours." When Mark put down two dimes, he shook his head. "You forget," he said, "for you, Doc, the price is only a nickel. But for you today, the coffee is for nothing." He made a half bow toward Arleen. "Treat for the lady from Barney, Doc."

Arleen smiled her thanks.

Two men came in and sat at the far end of the counter. The fan whirred overhead, but did nothing to dissipate the heat. Arleen thought of Neelie and the Luigui baby. She frowned. If it were hot in here, what was it like up there?

Mark was lifting his coffee cup to his lips. He said, "What's on your mind? The Luiguis?" There was an edge to his voice.

Arleen bit at her lip. "That poor baby," she said, "Think what it's like in that apartment." She frowned again. "A fan might help some."

Mark said sternly, "Don't go getting ideas. If you brought the Luiguis a fan, Anna or Tony would take it out and hock or sell it for what they could get, and use the money for wine. If the kids got to it first, they'd take it apart to see what made it run."

Arleen's voice shook. She was curiously angry at him. "And Neelie Ryan?" she said, "would her husband sell or pawn a fan if I brought her one?"

"No," he said. "But Miss Gibbons . . . she's the woman from the Welfare Department ("As if I don't know," Arleen thought) might not think a fan is necessary. And even if she approved, the landlord might not."

Arleen said stubbornly, "I'll pay the necessary electricity myself!"

Mark said quietly, "And would you pay for the electricity and fans for everyone on Leland Street, Arleen? Do you think the Ryans and the Luiguis are the only ones sweltering in their ugly, hot rooms?"

He shook his head, and his voice softened as he looked at her. "You have to develop a certain callousness," he told her, "because if you don't, you drop under the strain of it. You have to make yourself realize that you can't help them all; that you don't have the time or the money or the know-how to change things. So you plow along, helping as best you can, and yet always knowing that no matter how hard you work, you aren't going to change things for the majority

31

of them. If you succeed in changing the life of just one, that has to be reward enough."

Arleen stared at her coffee, not wanting it. The heat seemed to be coming up her back in slow, moist waves. She said, "There has to be some way. . . ."

Mark said gently, "Doesn't it say in the Bible, 'The poor you have always with you?'" He touched her arm. "Drink your coffee," he told her. "If you don't, Barney's feelings will be hurt."

Arleen drank the coffee. She and Mark left the heat of the restaurant for the heat of the street. They stood for a moment beside the little car.

Arleen said, frowning, "Mark, if you're so certain you aren't really helping these people, why do you stay here? Not for financial gain." She made a grimace. "Then why?"

The sadness she had glimpsed in his face in repose became even more evident. He said slowly, "Don't misunderstand me. I'm not saying I don't help them, because I do. And you do too. Only our help isn't going to change their way of life. We're deluding ourselves if we allow ourselves to think it's going to. First the cause must be found, and then the solution can begin."

He took a deep breath. "And as to why I keep an office here: I saw my mother die because we didn't have money enough for decent medical care for her. My father left us when I was three, because he wanted to be free. I determined that when I grew up, I was going to be a doctor and give my services to those who couldn't afford to pay for a decent doctor."

Arleen was deeply touched. She said softly, "I'm sorry, Mark."

He stared at her for a moment, brows knitted, and then he said, his voice brusque, "I expect I'd better give up on my philosophizing and let us both get back to doing our jobs."

With mixed emotions, Arleen watched him go. She was piqued by his brusqueness, that amounted almost to rudeness; touched to tender pity for the bitter, idealistic boy who had become the bitter, idealistic man.

Mark turned suddenly and glanced back at her, and there was something in his face. . . . Arleen was the first to look away. Her hands, turning the switch key, trembled.

She eased the coupé away from the curb. "Dr. Wynter is a fine man, a dedicated doctor," she told herself firmly. "I admire him for what he is. He is no more to me than that."

32

Arleen brought the fan for Neelie Ryan. A cool front had moved in, and Neelie didn't need the fan at the moment. But Arleen said firmly, "It isn't going to stay cool, and when it gets hot again you'll have the fan."

Neelie had an old magazine someone had brought her. She showed it to Arleen. "See that?" she said, her eyes shining. "That there's a picture of that Capistrano place. See all them swallows? Ain't they pretty? And all them flowers, ain't they nice? No wonder them swallows like to come back to that place."

She sighed and stared dreamily past the magazine. "The way I read, there's always flowers growing in California.·My, but wouldn't Al like that? He could grow himself flowers all the year round." She closed the magazine. "I'm going to fix that for my big chunk of happiness Al and me's entitled to. I'm just gonna say "Look, Lord, that's what I want for Al and me . . . that Capistrano place, and Al able to grow flowers anytime he wants to."

Arleen told herself unhappily that Neelie shouldn't do that, fix her mind on something like that. And then she thought fiercely, "Why not? What's wrong with it?"

Mark shook his head when she told him. The bitterness was strong around his mouth. "Poor Al," he said.

Arleen stared at him. "Poor Al?" she asked. "Why not poor Neelie? She's the one I'm concerned about. Al can get around. Neelie can't."

Mark said slowly, "You don't have to be concerned about Neelie. She's got inner reserves. Even when there's no future, she can still glimpse one; even without hope, she can hope. But Al's got only Neelie. He leans on her; she holds him up. She's his crutch; without her, he'd fall. Neelie would get up again if ever she fell. Al couldn't."

By the following week, the heat was back again with a vengeance. Evelyn Drew, home from the hospital, sailed her nurse's cap at the studio couch the moment she opened the door.

She ran her fingers through her blonde hair, causing it to stand up on end, and then began unbuttoning her uniform.

"I'm going to take a cold, cold, cold shower, and then lie down on that couch in my nothingness," she told Arleen.

Arleen grinned and shook her head. Clad in gay plaid Bermudas and a sleeveless blouse, she was sprawled on a chair close to the window fan, sipping a cold drink.

"You'll take your cold, cold, cold shower," she told Evelyn, "and then cover your nothingness before you lie

33

down on that particular couch. We have windows, my dearest darling, in case it has escaped you. And people sometimes come dashing in without knocking."

"And I," Evelyn wailed, "am hot, hot, hot!" She shrugged. "But as usual, my modest little friend, you are absolutely right."

She headed toward the bathroom, turned. "We had a friend of yours at the hospital this afternoon."

Arleen's head jerked up. "Friend?"

"One of the Luiguis," Evelyn said.

"Anna?" Arleen asked. She frowned.

Evelyn shook her head. "A Pietro Luigui," she said. "He ran out in the street and fell down in front of a car. The driver was so upset he put him into the car and brought him to the hospital. There wasn't a scratch on the boy, except a skinned knee where he'd fallen." She grinned. "But we had to give him a bath before we could be sure. I never saw so much dirt in my life. It was positively caked on him!"

Arleen said, "How did he ever let nurses close enough to him to give him a bath?"

"It was a job," Evelyn admitted. "It took two student nurses to hold him down, and one to give him a bath. The poor kids, they were soaked when it was finished." She pushed one hand through her hair again. "Man, talk about hot!" She narrowed her eyes on Arleen. "I gathered Pietro doesn't exactly like women. He's afraid of them." She laughed. "One of the interns, witty chap, said he completely sympathized with the poor kid . . . that he knew exactly how he felt."

Arleen said, "Pietro has an eruption on his skin. I thought it might be impetigo or ringworm, but I've never been able to get close enough to him to find out."

Evelyn shook her head. "The resident doctor thought it could be caused by a diet deficiency. He prescribed vitamins."

Arleen gave a harsh laugh. "They're on relief. Where's the money to come from?"

Evelyn shrugged. "If vitamins or medicine are prescribed by a doctor, wouldn't Welfare have to take care of the expense? After all, wouldn't they be as much a necessity as food?"

"Well, I guess you're probably right," Arleen agreed. Her lips tightened. "I'd like to put that child on a farm," she said, "where he could have, for once in his life, all of the good, rich milk and cream and butter and eggs that he could eat!"

34

Mark's words came to her: "And would you pay for all the electricity and all the fans on Leland Street, Arleen?"

She said, with sudden sadness, "There wouldn't be enough farms to house all of the needing ones, would there?"

Evelyn shook her head. She was frowning. "You take it too seriously," she told Arleen. "After all, you didn't have a hand in making things the way they are, and it's not up to you to do anything about them."

She flashed Arleen a wry grin. "This is what you get for having too many coffees with that dedicated Dr. Wynter. I told you he was a kook."

She had finished unbuttoning her uniform, and now took it off and hung it over one arm. "Fix me one of those long, cold ones you're drinking, will you? I'll be out of the shower in a jiffy. And honey, what you're lacking is good, old-fashioned fun. That's my diagnosis. The prescription is some nice, wacky dates with some nice, wacky guys, and I'm going to see that the prescription is filled."

On Friday Evelyn said, her eyes shining, "Know that prescription I gave you? Well, it's going to be filled tomorrow night at the Alhambra. Dinner and dancing."

Arleen stared at her. The Alhambra was one of the more elaborate night spots in Saltboro. She'd had a few dates with nice young men, but not once had she been taken to the Alhambra.

Evelyn laughed at her expression. She seemed to be enjoying herself. "Sound nice?"

Arleen said, doubt in her voice, "I'm not sure."

"Oh, you don't need to worry," Evelyn assured her. "Guy Newman is a perfect gentleman. Charley's known him from way back (Charley was Evelyn's current steady), and if Charley says he's a gentleman, then he is. He's young, rich . . . Charley says he part owner of an airplane manufacturing company in some small California town. He's flying in tomorrow morning for ten days. He's got some kind of business deal pending with a Detroit firm, Charley said. I told Charley I'd fix him up with a date."

Arleen had an odd feeling. Wasn't it funny that this blind date of hers should be from California, Neelie Ryan's dream place?

She dismissed the idea with an impatient shrug. What was she trying to make out of a mere coincidence? A lot of people came from California. It was a big state.

"So get out your best bib and tucker, honey," Evelyn told her gaily. "Saturday night's going to be a big night in your life."

Neither of them knew exactly how big.

CHAPTER 6

GUY NEWMAN was the gentleman Charley Purvis had said he was. In his early thirties, he was mildly attractive, pleasant company, and he danced well.

He held Arleen too close as they danced. Unobtrusively but firmly, she pushed herself out of his arms as they danced past the orchestra.

His arms loosened. "Sorry," he said. His blue eyes swept her face. "I don't have the wrong impression," he told her, "it's just . . . just—" he grinned, boyishly—"you're the most attractive girl I think I've ever met." Arleen blushed and looked down at the gleaming dance floor. She never had known how to handle a compliment smoothly.

It was air-conditioned at the Alhambra and Arleen felt cool and comfortable in her gay scarlet chiffon, with the glittering sequin combs nestling like stars in her dark hair.

Evelyn had nodded her approval earlier in the evening. "You look very snazzy. Not at all like your usual dull, demure self." She had grinned teasingly at Arleen. "Build your reputation on what you look like tonight, honey," she had advised her lightly.

The dance finished and Guy said urgently, "Let's step outside on the terrace, Arleen."

The Alhambra boasted a long terrace, banked with potted plants, and wooden planters bearing both real and artificial flowers. Arleen nodded. Guy's hand was loose but firm on her elbow. From the moment they were introduced, he'd made it clear that she was "Arleen" to him.

He had hair that hovered somewhere between blond and very light brown, and a boyish sprinkling of freckles across a slightly too large nose.

"You're not the 'Miss' type," he'd told Arleen. "Some girls are, you know. It seems unthinkable to call them anything except 'Miss something or other.'" He had sounded very serious about it. "So it's Arleen. I'm a man of strong

36

opinions," he'd added, grinning at her slightly startled look.

The terrace was filled with sweet, summery smells from the real flowers in the planters. The sky was filled with stars, and the night was black and rich and soft as an eiderdown quilt.

Guy took one of Arleen's hands and held it between two rough, hard palms. Arleen made no attempt to draw away. They perched on the edge of the railing. Lights of cars going or coming flashed occasionally in the parking lot. The muted sounds of traffic moving on the highway could be heard.

Unexpectedly, Guy said, "Have you ever been to California?

"No," Arleen said, shaking her head. She watched the blinking lights of a big jet plane cutting across the sky. And then she asked, "Have you ever seen Capistrano?" And was startled that the question had been so close to the surface of her mind.

"Capistrano? You mean the mission at Capistrano?" There was surprise in his voice.

"Yes," Arleen said. "Have you seen the swallows come back in the spring?"

He laughed. "No," he said. "We save that for the tourists."

There was a touch of coldness in Arleen's voice. "You make it sound as if it's something laughable."

"Laughable?" Guy said. He was suddenly serious. "No, I wasn't meaning it that way at all. It's just . . . well, it's there, and because it's there, no one actually thinks of going to see it."

His eyes probed hers. "How many people in New York go to see the Statue of Liberty? How many people in Philadelphia bother with Independence Hall? How many people in Detroit have seen the Henry Ford museum? And yet people travel from all over just to see these particular sights."

Arleen frowned. "What you're saying is that if something is within your reach, it loses its value for you?"

Guy said, "Something like that."

He still held her hand. There was a sudden, pulsating silence between them. Music from the orchestra inside drifted to them through the opened doors. There was the sound of laughter; of low, soft voices; the clink of glasses.

Guy said carefully, "Is there anyone special?"

Arleen knew he was asking about a special boy friend. She shook her head. "No."

He said, "Then the field's wide open?"

"Wide open," Arleen said lightly. Her hand moved inside

37

his, seeking release, like an imprisoned bird. He let her go.

"Have you ever thought about marriage?" he asked her.

Arleen said carefully, "It's a very nice institution. For those who like that sort of thing."

"What have you got against it?" he asked, his voice as careful as hers.

"Falling in love," she said, attempting to carry it off with a laugh and a shrug.

"I gather you were in love once," he said. "Over?"

Arleen nodded, a slight hardness in her voice. "A long time ago. He . . . didn't happen to love me. Not the way I loved him."

She swung away from the railing. Guy followed her. He caught her and forced her gently around to face him. "You're afraid of love," he told her, "and you shouldn't be." His voice was soft and low as a whisper against her cheeks. "Why, if you were my girl and I loved you . . ."

"Please," Arleen said, in a frantic voice. "I don't want to talk about it." She pulled herself free of his hands.

"All right," he said. His eyes swept her face. "But one of these days we're going to talk about it."

Arleen quickly changed the subject. "Have you always lived in California?" Her voice sounded quick and hurried and desperate to her ears.

Guy Newman followed her lead. He said, in a quiet, conversational tone, "All my life." He gave a wry grin. "Oh, not where I now live, nor in the exact manner in which I now live." He turned from Arleen and lit a cigarette. "Mind?"

She shook her head. In a vague way, she thought, Guy Newman reminded her of Mark Wynter. It was something she couldn't quite put her finger on.

"I lived in the slums as a boy. It was pretty squalid." He caught Arleen's look, and laughed. "Didn't you think the lovely state of California had slums? Slums, like the poor, are always with us. I've never been to Alaska, but I'm sure even there they have slums."

His boyish face was suddenly bleak. "It takes some doing to climb your way out of the slums," he said slowly. "It's like a deep pit, oiled and smooth all the way to the top. There's got to be a helping hand reached down to you. And you've got to have to want to climb out, inch by inch, or not all of the helping hands in the world are enough."

He drew in on his cigarette, and his eyes looked past Arleen into the lighted room beyond. "I had the want," he said, with a fierceness Arleen had not glimpsed in him before. "And I was given the helping hand.

"It was a young minister—a 'do gooder,' they called him. A friend of his owned a delicatessen. He got me a job in the store." Guy shook his head wryly. "It wasn't easy," he said. "I let him down time after time. I took money from the till; sometimes, if I felt especially bitter about life, I didn't even bother going to the store. But he never gave up holding onto my hand, and I inched my way up and out of the pit."

He gave an embarrassed laugh and flicked the cigarette off into the darkness. "Sorry," he said. "I guess I got wound up. No more Horatio Alger, Junior, stuff. I promise."

The orchestra was playing a waltz. He put his arms around her and danced her smoothly across the stone floor of the terrace. "Do you like Strauss?" he asked her.

Arleen nodded, and he said, "That's something we have in common. I also like California in June . . . Mendelssohn's wedding tune . . . hot dogs and banana splits . . . spritz . . ." He eyed her with humorous gaiety. "What's spritz? At least it rhymes. Now how about you?"

Arleen laughed, but said, quite seriously, "I'm glad you told me."

He was deliberately light. "About the rigors of my youth? I honestly don't burst out into the story of my life to attractive young ladies the first time I take them out. I don't know what got into me. I can't blame it on the drinks, because I haven't drunk that much."

Arleen said, with utmost sincerity, "I'm glad you talked to me about it. I really am. I feel as if now I know you."

Guy's arm tightened just the slightest. He said, huskily, "I'd like you to know me much, much better."

The music ended. Inside, there was the sound of the dancers returning to their tables. There was a moment of intense silence between Arleen and Guy, and then he said, his voice oddly shaky, "I'd like to kiss you, Arleen. I know it isn't exactly the proper thing to ask a girl like you on a first date, but I don't always follow the proper procedure. And I'd very much like to kiss you."

Arleen hesitated. It wasn't that she was prudish. . . . A pulse beat alarmingly in her throat. "Am I afraid to let him kiss me?" she asked herself fiercely, and as if in answer to the question, she lifted her face up to him, and closed her eyes.

It was a nice kiss. His lips were very pleasant, but no

more than that. The kiss did not stir up even a tiny flicker of excitement in her.

Not since Johnny. . . . She swallowed hard. It was much, much better this way.

Guy Newman stared down into her eyes. "Well, that's that," he said, a shade of regert in his voice. He touched her hand lightly. "I want to see you again."

He was good company, and a nice, safe person to be with, Arleen thought, and then realized that Guy Newman would hate knowing he was labeled under such a heading.

She nodded. "I'd like that very much."

Neelie Ryan had her fan going that Friday morning when Arleen made her usual end-of-the-week rounds. The flowers were blooming in their window boxes. And although the room was far from comfortable, even with the fan, it could have been worse.

Neelie was cheerful, as usual. "Ain't it nice?" she said, motioning toward the fan. "Miss Gibbons said it was all right about the fan; that she's glad you got it for me." She frowned in concentration. "You know, I'll bet Miss Gibbons' job ain't a bed of roses, with folks always saying how mean and stingy she is. Well, I got to thinking. She's got a boss, too, and she has to explain how come she gives this much money here, and this much money there. I guess in a job like that you'd have to learn to be hard, or folks would go taking advantage of you."

Arleen nodded. "You're very generous, Neelie, and I'm sure you're right about Miss Gibbons."

As Arleen left the building, she was frowning. How did an environment like Leland Street breed a Neelie Ryan and an Anna Luigui? What was the subtle ingredient in a person's makeup that provided one with cheerful acceptance, the other with sullen defeat?

What was it Mark Wynter had said of Neelie? That she had hope where wasn't hope . . . saw a future when there wasn't a future. Arleen sighed. If only that attitude could be injected like an antibiotic into all of the hopeless and defeated.

As she walked toward her car, she saw the blond boy with the elaborate hairdo whom she knew now to be one of the Roosters. He was alone, pushing with the toe of one pointed shoe at something in the gutter. He glanced up idly at Arleen, but made no move to cross the street.

Arleen had her hand on the door handle and was ready

to climb into the car when she saw what it was the boy was pushing at in the gutter. It was a bedraggled sparrow, making weak moves to escape. The boy would let him go so far, and then, like a cat with a mouse, he would push it back toward the curb and hold it there with his foot.

All of Arleen's instincts of human compassion for something weak and helpless came to the surface. She forgot to be afraid of the boy.

Her hand left the car door and she raced swiftly and indignantly across the street. She said, with fierce, cold anger, "Let that bird alone! What kind of a boy are you, to want to harm something so little and helpless as a bird?"

He raised his head and looked at her out of cruel, heavy-lidded eyes. Then deliberately he ground the bird's tiny legs under his heel. When he lifted his foot the bird lay there, not yet dead.

"Hey, nurse," the boy said, with mocking insolence, "ain't you gonna do something for the poor thing? You just gonna let it lay suffering like that?"

Arleen was shocked into immobility for a brief spell. Then one hand swooped downward and she lifted the bird gently and held it in the palm of her hand.

The boy waited, thumbs hooked insolently in the pockets of his tight jeans. "Well, doll?" he said.

Arleen could no longer look at him. Anger was a pain in her stomach, a burning, nagging pain against which she was helpless. The boy wanted to goad her on; that was why he had done this. She struggled against her anger, and with sudden resolution she turned around and walked back to the car.

She was hardly behind the wheel when she glimpsed Al Ryan shuffling his way toward the apartment building. She got quickly out of the car and went to him, holding out the bird.

She said, frantically, "Please finish killing it! Please!"

Al's eyes were slightly bloodshot; his mouth was loose. He looked at her, and then at the bird she held, as if trying to take everything in.

He took the bird when Arleen pushed it desperately at him, turned it over in his hand, then looked up at Arleen. "Whata you mean, finish killing it? This bird's already dead."

Tears rolled down Arleen's cheeks. She was no longer able to hold them back. Al Ryan handed her the dead bird, stared down at his hands and continued shuffling his way toward the building.

Arleen drew an unsteady breath. She thought, "I shouldn't have allowed myself to lose my dignity like that." Across the street, she knew the blond boy still waited. Her stomach knotted. She could not leave the bird here, even though the boy could no longer harm it.

Later, she laid the bird gently on the grass at the end of the sweep of lawn in front of the county-city building. Her hands were sticky from its blood. She went inside, down to the basement where the restrooms were, and washed carefully.

The nagging pain of anger did not leave her, and that night when she went to bed it still haunted her.

Evelyn took it philosophically. "The bird would have died anyway; it was probably injured when that boy found it. You don't want to take on so about these things, Arleen."

But it wasn't the bird, Arleen knew—even if Evelyn didn't. It was that the boy could have wantonly injured it merely for the pleasure it gave him to see Arleen get aroused. She shuddered, and although the room was blisteringly hot she felt chilled.

CHAPTER 7

ON SATURDAY she went again to the Alhambra with Guy Newman. Evelyn and Charley did not accompany them this time.

Arleen had protested that Guy did not have to spend the kind of money on her that the Alhambra cost. "We could go to an air-conditioned movie," she told him, "and have hamburgers and malts afterward. I'd have just as good a time."

Guy said teasingly, "If I were going to take you to a movie, it would be a drive-in. 'Passion pits'—isn't that what the kids call them? And I'd be wasting my money. We never would know whether or not the movie was any good, because we wouldn't be seeing it." Then he added, in sudden seriousness, "Money is one thing I have. There are some things I lack, such as a family . . . closeness . . . but not money."

Arleen was dancing with him when suddenly he stopped,

pushed her slightly away from him, and stared down at her. "Why so pensive tonight?"

Arleen gave a wry smile. "I'm sorry," she said, "but something happened yesterday that I just can't seem to put out of my mind." And she told him about the episode.

Guy said slowly, "A bully in the slums is no different from a bully in the higher-class neighborhoods, except perhaps there are more of them in the slums."

He pulled her to him again, his hand warm and gentle on her waist. He said, with sudden savagery, "You shouldn't be doing the sort of work that exposes you to that kind of ugliness."

Arleen said quietly, "Guy, I'm a nurse. I'm not doing this kind of work because I have to, but because I want to."

"You should be some man's wife. You should have a man to protect you and take care of you."

Arleen, not liking the direction the conversation was taking, quickly changed the subject. She was almost feverishly gay, and yet she managed to keep a wall of aloofness between herself and Guy.

He was ruefully aware of it. He said, "A man can climb a mountain that's never been climbed, jump a seemingly impossible chasm, and yet if the lady doesn't give a darn. . . ." He shrugged. "I'm a guy who enjoys butting his head against steel bars just to see if he can break through. I'm leaving for Detroit in the morning, and flying back to Altrua in the evening. It will probably be six weeks before I'll be coming back here. Will you save me an evening?"

Arleen nodded. She said, "I'm going to miss you." The knowledge surprised her. She really was going to miss him.

His eyes searched hers. "Me?" he asked. "Or this?" Waving his hand around the softly lighted, expensively simple room.

Arleen flushed, and said chidingly, "You should know the answer to that, Guy."

He conceded that he did. His smile was a small boy's smile. "I just wanted to hear you put it into words," he told her. "That you really are going to miss me. Me, personally."

It was 1:10 when he cupped her chin with one hand, turned her face toward him, and bent to kiss her good night. He would have stretched out the kiss, but Arleen gently but firmly drew away.

43

"Good night, Guy," she said in a steady voice, her eyes watching him warily.

He seemed to have decided to give the situation the light treatment. "A lovely moonlit night, and you don't feel romantic?"

He bent toward her, touched a tendril of hair, wound it about one finger, then drew back his hand. "That evening I asked you to save for me," he told her. "I didn't really mean just one evening, Arleen, but all of them."

Arleen laughed and said with careful lightness, "Why, Guy, weren't you taught that it's not polite to be grabby?"

She was surprised when she received his phone call on Sunday night.

"Arleen? I'm at Detroit Metropolitan. I had the sudden, uncontrollable urge to hear your voice. Do you mind very much?"

"Mind?" Arleen said. "I should be complimented."

"*Are* you complimented?" he asked.

"Yes," she said. "Of course I am."

Evelyn was regarding her gravely when she hung up and turned from the phone.

"Guy Newman?" When Arleen nodded, she said, "Did you know he's in love with you?"

"That's not true!" Arleen protested. "We've had a few dates; they've been fun. I know he likes me. I like him, too. But that's not love!" She felt distressed.

Evelyn shrugged. "Tell Guy that," she said lightly.

Arleen lay awake for a long time that night. She did not want Guy Newman to be in love with her, because she was not in love with him. She would not allow herself to be in love with any man. Love was a pain no one wanted to feel again, if he were wise.

The sky was gray and overcast, and a chill breeze was blowing, when she awakened next morning. It seemed impossible that the day before had been swimming weather. As she walked to her car she glanced at the thermometer on the outside of the building. It said 54 degrees. On Sunday it had registered 91.

Neelie Ryan was sitting up in bed when Arleen walked into the room, and Al Ryan, a sweater pulled over his shirt, was working on his plants.

Neelie looked up with her usual smile. "You bring this weather, Miss Anderson?"

Arleen laughed. "One thing you can say about Michigan weather: it certainly isn't monotonous."

"Al's worried about some of his plants," Neelie said. "He's afraid they're starving to death for lack of plant food."

Arleen frowned. She was on the verge of asking why, if that were so, he didn't buy some plant food, when she stopped herself from framing the question. It took money to buy plant food, and Welfare certainly was not going to supply money for such a cause. And if Al made a few quarters he'd use the money to buy wine, even though he was very fond of his flowers.

He said, instead, "How much does plant food cost?"

Neelie shook her head. "My, I wouldn't be knowing that exactly. Not very much, I don't think."

When she had finished taking care of Neelie, Arleen pressed two one-dollar bills into her hand. She said, "I think it will buy enough plant food."

Neelie said, shaking her head, "Oh, no, Miss Anderson, we can't let you do that. I wasn't meaning . . . I wasn't asking you for the money." She looked distressed and upset.

Arleen said, "I know you weren't, Neelie. I want to do this." She squeezed the woman's hand. "I like seeing your flowers when I come here, Neelie. It's the bright spot in my day." She frowned suddenly. "You and your flowers, Neelie, are my morale boosters."

Al Ryan turned to face her. He said, harshly, "Take your money back, Miss Anderson. We can get along without it!"

Arleen said, her voice cold and stern, "It isn't for you, Mr. Ryan. It's for the plants."

Before she left, she said to Neelie, "I had a few dates with someone from California. He lives about fifty miles from the mission at Capistrano."

Neelie looked interested. "My," she said, wistfully, "that must be grand."

Arleen shook her head. "He's lived all of his life in California, Neelie, and he's never once visited the mission."

"My," Neelie said, as if it were incomprehensible to her. And then, "Well, I guess we can't all like the same things, can we? It would be a pretty dull world if we did."

Arleen thought, ruefully, as she left the Ryans', how queer the world was run. Guy Newman had Neelie's dream at his fingertips, and it had no meaning for him. And Neelie in all probability would never see her dream come true.

There was a tightening pressure in Arleen's chest as she walked down the stairs. She no longer had to visit the

Luiguis. Anna was entirely on her own. She thought about Carmella, and wondered if she were being kept clean, dry, fed. Carmella was such a pretty baby.

Well, Arleen thought, as she passed the Luigui apartment, there was nothing she could do about it. She couldn't force herself into these people's lives.

She hesitated. Anna must be reminded to go for her six weeks' check-up soon. She wouldn't go, of course, but it was required that she be told.

Arleen turned and walked back down the hall. She could tell Anna now about the check-up, and it would afford her an opportunity to see how Carmella was coming along.

The little girl to whom she'd given the candy bar that first day opened the door to her, and stared, wide-eyed and dirty-faced, up at her.

Arleen said gently, "Is your mother home?"

The little girl's head moved slowly back and forth. Arleen stepped inside the door. "I'd like to see Carmella," she said. "Is she asleep?"

The child shook her head again. Arleen followed her to the sagging, dirty bed on which the baby lay. Arleen's heart gave a lurch. The baby was dirty. Arleen felt her. She was wet, too. Arleen bent down and lifted the baby gently in her arms. She was also hungry, Arleen surmised.

She knew it was useless to wonder if there were any formula made up for the baby. She looked at the wide-eyed little girl standing in front of her and regarding her solemnly.

"What's your name?" she asked her.

"Angela," the child said, and popped a dirty thumb between her lips.

"Well, Angela," Arleen said, "Do you think you could go to the store for me and get some canned milk for Carmella?"

Angela nodded.

Arleen smiled at her. "I'll write it down for you, just in case you can't remember." She handed Angela the note and a dollar. "Get some candy for yourself and your brothers and sisters," she told her. "Get enough so you'll all have some."

While Angela was gone, Arleen bathed and changed the baby. She held Carmella's soft body against herself and crooned, "You poor little thing. You poor little thing, you."

When Angela returned, Arleen made up a formula, filled a bottle, and fed the baby, who drank hungrily, and then, fed and clean, feel asleep in Arleen's arms.

Arleen laid down the baby, hugged Angela before she left.

"How is Pietro?" she asked her. She hadn't seen the little boy, and guessed he was hiding in the other room. "Does he take his vitamin pills?"

The little girl's head moved back and forth again. "They eat Pietro's candy," she said. "Pietro don't get none of it. They eat it up on him."

Arleen started to say, "But it isn't candy," and then changed her mind, knowing she'd only be wasting her breath.

Walking to her car, she thought, wryly philosophical, that at least the Luigui children were getting their vitamins.

She slid behind the wheel but did not turn on the switch key. "What am I waiting for?" she scolded herself. "For Dr. Mark Wynter to come along?"

She felt the flush stain her cheeks. There was no sense in lying to herself. It had been days since she and Mark had had coffee together, or even seen each other. She missed him. She more or less looked forward to seeing him, as she looked forward to seeing Neelie Ryan.

It wasn't as a man she missed him, she told herself fiercely. It was as a friend.

Suddenly aware of a terrible need for a cup of coffee, she turned the switch key and headed the car in the direction of Barney Bonardio's restaurant. She was honest with herself. "It's because I hope Mark will come in while I'm there."

Barney displayed a wide grin when she walked in the door. "Well, it is long time no see, Miss Anderson," he greeted her.

He polished the counter violently in front of Arleen when she sat down. "I've been terribly busy," she apologized. She ordered coffee, hesitated, then said, "And a hamburger."

He beamed on her. "Barney make you the best hamburger you ever tasted. You see." He was facing the front of the restaurant and the big window that looked on the street. "Too bad," he said, making a "tsking" sound with his lips. "I think—my wife she think—that Rose is somebody. She will make something of herself. But now. . . ." he shrugged. "Now she like all the other girls around here—no good."

He scraped the top of the grill with a spatula, and then patted a round of hamburger into a patty.

Arleen swung around on the stool to gaze out of the window. She glimpsed the back of Rose Luigui as she swung with studied insolence along the sidewalk.

Barney squashed down the hamburger savagely. He said, "Something ought to be done!" His voice was angry.

"About Rose Luigui?" Arleen asked him.

47

"About all of them!" he said fiercely. "About places like Leland Street. Something ought to be done!"

Arleen nodded. "I know," she said. "But how?"

"Yes," Barney said, slowly, "but how. That's it, Miss Anderson. But how. That's what stops people."

Suddenly he was his old, easygoing self. A wide grin split his face. "Hey," he said, "here comes doc. The lady's having a hamburger. You want one too, Doc?"

Mark shrugged, then nodded. "I'll take a chance, Barney. At least I can recognize the symtoms of ptomaine, so I won't be caught unawares." He turned his attention to Arleen. "Why, Miss Anderson," he said, "Arleen for short, I haven't seen much of you lately. I hear you have a boy friend."

Arleen said slowly, "I had a few dates with a man. I don't consider him my 'boy friend'."

"No?" Mark asked. "That's not the way I heard it."

"You heard wrong, then," Arleen informed him crisply.

Barney was grinning. "Hey, Doc," he said, "you jealous, huh? Well, I don't blame you. She's a very pretty woman."

"Jealous?" Mark said, scoffing at the idea. There was a faint flush on his face. He fumbled for his cigarettes, lit one, directed a teasing smile at Arleen, and said, "These romantic Italians!"

Arleen gave him back a smile. "We'll just ignore him," she said. To herself she denied the thought that Mark Wynter being jealous of her afforded her pleasure. "Why should it?" she asked herself calmly, "since I'm not interested in him except as a friend?"

CHAPTER 8

AL RYAN'S windowbox garden was in full, rich bloom by June. Arleen said, "It's like being in a country garden. Why, I can close my eyes and pretend I'm back home in Carson."

Neelie Ryan beamed. Even Al Ryan, discarding for a few moments his bitterness and defeat, seemed to puff out with pride at what his old fingers had accomplished with so little material.

"The plant food helped the weak plants," Neelie told Arleen. "They just seemed to spring right up after they got fed."

48

Al swung around and the old, tight anger was once again on his face. He said, "There was some change left after I bought the plant food, Miss Anderson. Want to know what I did with that change? Saved it to give back to you? Spent it on some little thing Neelie'd like? I bought myself a bottle of wine with it; that's what I did."

Neelie looked distressed. She regarded him anxiously. "Now, Al, what are you trying to do, make Miss Anderson think you're a bad man? She don't think that, no matter how much talk you give her. Do you, Miss Anderson?"

Arleen shook her head. "No," she said gently, her eyes on Neelie's anxious face. "Of course I don't think that. I know Al isn't a bad man." She turned and faced him. "A weak man, perhaps, but not a bad one."

It was a day of harsh, hot wind and blistering heat. Wind-blown street dust stabbed at Arleen's cheeks and stung her eyes. As she climbed into her car she saw Peter Rossi across the street, in front of the poolroom.

He gave her a blank stare and then looked away, his ignoring of her a kind of insult.

She was ready to drive away when she saw Mark Wynter coming along the street. She waited for him, her hands lying idly on the wheel.

"Hi," she said, when he was almost abreast of her.

He'd been staring at the street, seeming to be lost in reverie. At the sound of her voice he raised his head.

"Hi," he said. He moved over to the car. Across the street young Peter Rossi, lounging against the front of the brick building, gave a sudden start of interest.

"Keeping you busy?" Arleen asked.

Mark nodded. He looked tired, Arleen thought. "You, too?"

"Yes," Arleen said. And then, impulsively, "You look as if you don't get enough sleep. You've got to keep yourself well, you know, or you won't be any good to anyone."

She was astounded at her outburst. Her face reddened. "I'm sorry," she said awkwardly. "I must have sounded like your mother."

Mark shook his head. "My mother wouldn't have had that much interest. She was too sick herself to worry about me." He seemed to be regarding her with sudden, intent interest.

Arleen, feeling that the moment was awkward, said, "Have I a spot on my nose?"

He didn't grin. He said, his voice sounding stilted, like a young boy who's afraid he doesn't know the right words, "The Strand is air-conditioned. There's some kind of Western

49

playing there. If you don't mind Westerns, maybe we could take in a movie—if you wouldn't mind going with me, that is."

Arleen flushed. She said coldly, "Are you asking me to go out with you, Dr. Wynter?"

He frowned at her, his gray eyes narrowed. "I thought that was what I was doing."

"Did you?" Arleen asked him. She laughed at his discomfiture. "I guess that's what you did think." She pushed at a lock of brown hair that had fallen across one eye. "I happen to like Westerns very much," she said. "I'll be happy to go to the movies with you, Mark."

"I don't have a car."

"We can use mine."

He shook his head, his face stiff with pride. "When a girl goes with me, she rides the bus."

"All right," Arleen said, "so we ride the bus."

Mark seemed to loosen up. He said, grinning, "Peter Rossi is very interested in these proceedings. He's convinced I have absolutely no interest in the female sex except as patients. He's about to concede now that I may be human after all!" His eyes swept her face. He added slowly, "Peter doesn't understand that a man and a woman can just like each other . . . as friends."

A slow anger burned in Arleen as she drove back to the city-county building. Had Mark Wynter been warning her? Saying, "I like you as a friend, but don't try to crowd any closer than that?"

She was embarrassed at the thought, and her cheeks burned with humiliation. If only Mark Wynter knew how little he interested her, except as a friend!

They sat in the balcony at the Strand. Mark had provided two bags of popcorn. Around them, teenagers huddle in close embraces, giggled, occasionally gave deep, soul-reaching sighs.

Mark said, "It looks as if we're marooned in necker's heaven."

Arleen gave a nervous giggle. "It looks like that."

She wondered if Mark would try to hold her hand, touch her, and how she should react if he did. She needn't have worried. He kept a good safe distance from her.

When it was over, and they were outside again on the street, Mark said, with a laugh, "I notice the hero still rides a white horse."

"What else?" Arleen said, laughing too.

"Beer?" he asked, "or a malted?" They stood at the

curb, ready to cross, Mark's hand curved lightly just under Arleen's left elbow.

"Coffee," Arleen said.

There was only a sprinkling of people on the street. The movie house had been only partially filled, in spite of the air-conditioning.

They ended up having pizzas with their coffees, in a tiny, quiet restaurant that window fans fought to keep cool.

Watching Mark eat the pizza, which Arleen thought was remarkably good, she said, frowning, "I'll make a bet that pizza is your dinner."

Mark flushed; laughed it aside. "You'd win the bet," he told her.

Arleen pushed half of her pizza toward him. "I haven't touched it. I shouldn't have ordered it. I'm not at all hungry. And it's time I began thinking seriously about my weight."

Mark gave her a cold stare, and pushed back her plate across the table. "I'm not that poverty stricken," he said. "I was perfectly able to afford taking you out tonight or I'd never have asked you! I'm loaded with money—twenty-five dollars worth."

When Arleen looked blank, he gave a short laugh and said, "A man paid me part of a bill he's owed me for six months. Not in my wildest dreams did I imagine that I'd ever get the money."

A wry grin twisted the edges of his lips. "He put a two-dollar bet on a horse. A long shot. It came in and paid two hundred and forty dollars. He never forgot me. He was drunk when he came to my office, but he hadn't forgotten."

Suddenly he laughed out loud. Arleen thought how young and gay he looked when he laughed. "Want to know what the name of the horse was? 'Doc's Choice.'" He laughed again.

When he took her home, he stood staring down at her, and his hands pressed, with rough gentleness, into her shoulders. His gray eyes searched her face as if seeing it for the first time. Awkwardly he pulled her to him, and his lips touched hers, gently at first, then with fierce, rough passion.

As if suddenly realizing, his hands dropped from her shoulders and he stepped back away from her. "Sorry," he said. "I don't know what possessed me." His lips tightened. "You needn't worry that it will happen again."

Arleen found she was trembling, as she opened the door and walked into her own apartment. Not since Johnny had any man's kiss touched her as Mark Wynter's had.

She caught her breath sharply. She was not going to lose

her head over Mark Wynter; she'd learned her lesson. She was not likely to be fool enough to forget what she had learned!

Evelyn glanced up when Arleen walked in. She was sprawled in a chair, legs dangling over the side, reading. "Well," she said, "back early from the big date. You look flustered. Did the nice young doctor try to kiss you?"

When Arleen's flush deepened, Evelyn said, in great delight, "Hey, I think he not only tried, he succeeded! Well, what do you know about that? He's human. I'll have to spread the word!"

Arleen said fiercely, "If you dare to do a thing like that!"

Evelyn shook her head. "Oh, honey," she said, "you know I was only joking. But I'm saying this seriously . . . you'd better get those stars out of your eyes for Dr. Wynter, and if you're aching to lose your heart to someone, I might mention Guy Newman. Now there's a man who'll love back. By the way, he phoned you tonight."

"Guy?" Arleen said. "He's in California, isn't he?"

Evelyn nodded. "You're forgetting that telephone wires stretch from California."

"Why would he call me long distance?"

Evelyn shrugged. "I could tell you the real reason, but you wouldn't believe me. I told you before, he's in love with you."

Arleen said harshly, "Please!"

"You don't want to hear the truth, so I won't tell you. The excuse Guy gave is that he's flying into Detroit on some business tomorrow afternoon. He wants to see you tomorrow night."

"I don't know . . ." Arleen began.

"He said you promised him. You promised him all of your nights while he was in town."

Arleen looked upset. "I'm sure I didn't promise him that."

Evelyn sighed. "What's wrong with Guy? He's attractive, young, rich, and he's a real nice guy besides." Her eyes lit up. "Hey," she said, "that's a pun . . . I made a pun. 'A real nice Guy.' Get it?"

Arleen was in no mood for such lightness. When she went to bed it was as if a heavy load were pressing against her chest. She did not want Guy Newman to fall in love with her. She did not want it at all!

The next morning Dr. Rowe, who headed the health department, smiled down on her. "Miss Anderson," he said,

"I've been hearing very good reports about you. It seems, according to some people, that you're an angel in disguise."

Arleen blushed, and he laughed. Then he frowned. "You look too young for that area," he said. "I wonder. . . ."

Miss Horne, who was supervisor of the visiting nurses, overheard. She said, "Miss Anderson can take care of herself, Dr. Rowe. I'm sure we need have no worries on that score. And besides, Dr. Wynter is in that area." She turned toward Arleen. "You've met Dr. Wynter, haven't you?"

Arleen nodded, and Miss Horne's keen eyes moved across her face and then away again, quickly.

Dr. Rowe said, chewing on a cigar, "He's a fine doctor, Mark Wynter is. I can't understand why he's starving himself to death. If he opened an uptown office he'd have more patients than he could handle." He ground the cigar out in an ash tray. "The man's an utter fool!"

Miss Horne said softly, "He's a dedicated man, Dr. Rowe. Is that synonymous with fool?"

"I really don't know, Miss Horne. I really don't know."

The Luigui baby was on Arleen's mind. On impulse she stopped in at the Welfare office. Miss Gibbons was there. She glanced up when Arleen walked in.

There was a sardonic ring to her voice. "And what are you searching for this morning, Miss Anderson? A sea cruise for some of my Welfare clients?"

Arleen said steadily, "I'm worried about the Luigui baby, Miss Gibbons. I know Welfare provides food for the child, but I don't think she's getting the proper amount of milk. The last time I stopped in I found the mother gone and the baby alone except for the younger children. The baby was wet, dirty and hungry."

Miss Gibbons gave her a cold glance. "Are you suggesting the infant be taken from the home and placed, Miss Anderson?"

Arleen shook her head. "I'm only suggesting that a tiny baby needs care and food, Miss Gibbons."

The Welfare visitor's face dropped suddenly. She shook her head, the sternness gone for the moment. She said, "We can provide an existence for such people, but we can't give them the real necessity of life—the want to do more than exist."

She shrugged, and the coldness was back in her face. "The other Luiguis were raised the same way this one is being brought up. It's all they know. And they've survived. Things

53

that would kill a child reared in a different environment don't faze these people."

She shook her head at Arleen. "You think little Carmella Luigui should be loved. I think that, too, but we aren't the child's mother, Miss Anderson. The child's mother doesn't recognize the existence of love. It is sex to her, the begetting of a child she does not want, ugliness."

Arleen turned to go. Miss Gibbons said softly, "There's nothing to stop you from looking in on the baby when you're in the building, Miss Anderson. Mrs. Luigui blusters, but she's afraid of people she thinks are in authority. A visit from you might keep her more in line when it comes to taking care of the baby."

Arleen nodded. "Yes, Miss Gibbons." She thought, "She isn't really hard. She's had to grow callous, as Mark said, because otherwise she couldn't live with her work. Will I grow callous too?" she wondered. "Will I have to become like that?"

She paused outside the Luigui's door, and then her hand rapped sharply. There was no sound except the fretful wailing of a small baby.

Arleen rapped again, louder this time. She called out, "Mrs. Luigui, it's the visiting nurse. Please let me in."

When there was no answer, and the baby's wails grew louder and more insistent, Arleen turned the knob and walked inside, and nearly fell over Anna Luigui's sprawled body.

CHAPTER 9

Anna's mouth was open and she was breathing heavily. Her head was thrown back, her body twisted grotesquely. Arleen knelt, felt for a pulse, and found it strong and steady.

She leaned back on her heels and considered the possibilities. From the odor on her breath, it was obvious that Anna had been drinking. She could have staggered, fallen down, hit her head on the table leg. She could be in coma from the effect of the fall, or she could be unconscious merely as a result of her drinking.

Whichever it was, it was not Arleen's place to guess at a diagnosis. Carmella was sobbing pitifully. Arleen went over and picked up the baby. Even Carmella's little feet were wet.

With a tender cry, Arleen took a large towel from her bag and wrapped it around the baby. She frowned down at Anna, and thought, "While I delay here, Anna could be seriously injured and in need of immediate medical attention." She was impatient with herself. Had she forgotten her function as a nurse?

Clutching the baby against her, she hurried out into the hall in search of someone to send for Dr. Wynter. There was no telephone in the building. To find a public telephone, phone the Health Department and arrange for a department doctor to be sent to Mrs. Luigui would take too much precious time, if Anna were seriously injured.

Gazing about the street for someone to send on the errand, Arleen saw Peter Rossi leaning against a lamppost, within hearing distance of her voice. When he raised his head and gave her his usual blank stare, she motioned frantically for him to come to her. He hesitated, then, with careful insolence, strutted toward her.

Carmella was making little whimpering, unhappy sounds. Arleen rocked her gently in her arms. She looked up at Peter Rossi and said worriedly, "It's Mrs. Luigui. I found her unconscious on the floor. I'm afraid she needs a doctor. Would you go to Dr. Wynter's office and ask him to come?"

Peter stared at her, and then he began to laugh harshly. "You kiddin'? Me tramp clear over to Doc's office for that old dame? You don't need to worry about her. Her and Tony were out drinking last night. She's just sleeping it off."

Arleen frowned. "Tony . . . that's Mr. Luigui, isn't it? Do you know where he is?"

The boy shrugged. "Who knows? Who cares? Sleeping it off in some gutter, maybe."

Carmella's whimpers were louder now. Arleen said, frantically, "The baby is wet and hungry, and Mrs. Luigui is in there alone. Will you please do as I asked you? Get Dr. Wynter to come, even though you don't approve of my summoning help for Mrs. Luigui."

Peter scowled at her. "Dames!" he said. But he swung around and walked down the street in the direction of Mark's office.

Arleen called after him, "Please, tell him to hurry."

She found a blanket and spread it over Anna Luigui. It was sticky with dirt, but it was the best Arleen could find. She eased a pillow under Anna's head. It was all she could do for her until Mark arrived.

Anna's pulse was still strong and steady, and she appeared to be snoring. More and more Arleen suspected Peter Rossi was right, and Anna's unconsciousness could be attributed solely to the excessive amount of alcohol in her system. She grinned to herself. "I used a lot of words to say I think Anna Luigui is plain drunk!"

She searched the littered apartment for diapers, but they seemed nonexistent. She folded a towel from her bag, used that to diaper the baby. Then she sponged off the small face and hands, the thin, bony chest. She powdered the baby, using an extra amount of talcum powder, then hugged Carmella to her. "There now," she said, "you smell sweet and nice."

She washed out a bottle, found an opened can of milk that seemed fresh. She tasted it, decided it was all right, fixed Carmella a bottle. She had just finished and was feeding the baby when Peter opened the door and strolled in. He looked, without any real interest, at Anna lying on the floor.

"Doc's pretty busy right now, sewing up some old dame who got herself cut. He said he'd be over as soon as he finished."

He stepped over to look down at Anna. "For an old dame, she sure can drink!" His nose wrinkled with disgust. "Man, man," he said, "I thought my old lady was a crazy housekeeper, but that was before I saw this pad!"

There was a shrill sound from the doorway, and Rose Luigui's voice said sharply, "Listen, little man, you don't like it here, you just go. Hear? Nobody says you have to stay. Nobody said you had to come!"

Peter's dark face flushed. "Listen, doll," he said, "I go when I want. And I don't like that 'little man' jazz."

Rose planted both hands on her hips. She stood, one shoulder raised slightly higher than the other, regarding him mockingly, "Lonnie Michos says you're a little man, Peter. He says he don't think you're big enough to lead the Roosters."

Peter's lips tightened. "Lonnie Michos is a punk," he said. "He don't know from nothing."

Rose's gaze grew even more mocking. "You're going to have to prove that, maybe, little man."

Peter's eyes narrowed. "I'll prove it," he said. "And no more of that 'little man' stuff, doll."

Rose took her hands from her hips. She shrugged. "Sure," she said, "if you say so."

Peter flushed. "Listen, doll—" he began.

Arleen, who had listened to the clash between the two, said sharply, "Rose, that's your mother lying there on the floor. You haven't shown any concern for her. You haven't even asked if she's hurt."

Rose laughed and flashed a scornful look down at her mother. "The old lady's drunk," she said. "It's not unusual."

Arleen said, shocked, "She could have hit her head against something when she fell. She could have injured herself."

"So she could have injured herself. What am I supposed to do, cry my little old eyes out? What's she ever done for me, except let me be born? And as for that part of it, she needn't have bothered."

Peter Rossi said, in a harsh, tight voice, "Amen. That goes for my old lady, too."

Arleen saw the way the two of them looked at each other with sudden interest, as if seeing each other for the first time.

She laid Carmella down. When she straightened again she saw Mark Wynter walking in the door. He strode over to Anna, knelt on one knee beside her, and reached for her wrist.

Arleen said, "I found her pulse strong and steady, Doctor."

Mark nodded. He listened to Anna's chest and heart, probed with experienced fingers the back of her neck under the dark, tangled hair.

Then he rose to his feet. "I'd say the lady has imbided too much. Other than that, I can find no contusions or abrasions." He grinned slightly. "Not even a scratch." He looked at Peter Rossi. "I think the two of us can lift her onto a bed."

Rose said harshly, "Why don't you just let her stay where she is? She must have liked that particular part of the floor or she wouldn't have laid down there in the first place."

Mark ignored her and nodded at Peter Rossi. "You take her feet, Peter."

There was no sheet on the bed. Arleen spread a tattered blanket over the mattress before they laid Anna on it, then looked at the woman on the bed. She said, "If I sponged her face and arms it might help."

Rose gave a tight, hard laugh. "You can't get soap and water on her when's she sober," she told Arleen, "so you're going to take advantage of her when she's drunk!" She shook her head. "Poor Ma. She's real attached to that dirt, too."

Mark said sharply, "Heat Miss Anderson some water, and be quick about it."

Arleen was amazed to see Rose flash him a scowl, but move off to do his bidding. Arleen bathed Anna's face, her shoulders, her arms and hands. Rose brought her a comb, and she combed a semblance of order into the tangled mass of hair.

Peter Rossi had watched with frowning interest from the doorway. He said, "I thought nurses gave medicine and shots, that kind of stuff. I didn't know they had to take care of drunken dames, give them baths, clean up messy kids." He seemed nonplused and confused.

Arleen said slowly, "I'm a visiting nurse, Peter. I go into areas where a nurse is needed, and I do what needs to be done. Sometimes it's giving a shot. Sometimes it's washing out clean diapers for a baby when the mother is unable to do it."

Peter shook his head. "Crazy," he said. "Crazy."

When Arleen looked up again, he was gone. Finished with Anna, she looked to make certain that Carmella was still sleeping. When she turned around, Mark was at her elbow.

His eyes held a queer, intent look. He said, "You looked like a mother gazing down on her own baby."

Arleen sighed. "Oh, Mark," she said, "they need love so desperately. Even Rose." Her lips quivered. "Maybe Rose most of all."

Mark said sharply, "Didn't I tell you that you had to learn to be callous?" He gave her shoulders a gentle shake. "It's the only way you can live with this!"

"Well, now," Rose Luigui's mocking voice said from behind them, "am I interrupting something interesting?"

Arleen flushed, but Mark said calmly, "Rose, I want you to stay here with Carmella. I don't want her left alone. Your mother shouldn't be left alone, either." His gaze probed her face. "Where's your father?"

Rose shrugged. "How would I know? My old man's at home even less than my old lady."

Mark's voice sharpened. "You're old enough to see that your brothers and sisters are fed, and be at home yourself instead of running in the streets." He waved a hand around the filthy room. "And old enough to see that this pigpen is kept livable. If your mother won't do it, then you must."

"Yeah?" she said belligerently. "Who said so? I ain't the mother here. That's Ma's job. She asked for it!"

Mark said, carefully, "Do you want Carmella to die from neglect, Rose?"

The girl looked frightened suddenly, and young, and anxious. "No," she said. "But I'm not supposed to. . . ."

Mark didn't let her finish. "All right, then," he said, "see that she's taken care of. And tell your mother for me that unless I see some improvement in her housekeeping, and in the care of her children, I'm going to see that the Welfare office receives a notation from me that you children would be better off taken from the home and placed. Tell her that if the children are taken away from her, her Welfare checks will stop. Both your mother and father are strong and able to work. Without the children your mother will be required to work."

Rose laughed coldly. "I'll tell her, Doc. That's a bad word to Ma—'work.' "

Downstairs, Arleen looked up at Mark. "Can you do that?" she asked him. "Ask that the children be taken from the home?"

Mark shrugged. "I can ask it," he said, "but Welfare's doing it is something else again. There's a philosophy among certain people that maintaining a child in its own home is best. Maybe the philosophy is based on the fact that there aren't enough homes to house all of the ones who should be taken away from their own parents."

Arleen sighed. "I never realized before I came to Saltboro that people had to contend with this terrible kind of poverty."

Mark's eyebrows lifted. "You were fortunate," he said. "You should have stayed where· life was safe and secure, Miss Anderson. It would have been much easier for you."

Arleen said coldly, "Dr. Wynter, if I had wanted life to be safe and secure, I wouldn't have picked out nursing as a career—especially not this particular kind of nursing."

His gray eyes swept her face; warmed. "Forgive me," he said. "Sometimes I find myself taking out my anger at my own inadequacies on others."

Arleen looked at him. "Inadequate? You? Dr. Rowe, at the Health Department, told me that if you had an office uptown, you'd have more patients than you could handle. He says you're a fine doctor, Mark."

Mark lifted one eybrow. It gave him a slightly sardonic look. "Well, I must thank Dr. Rowe for such kind words, however undeserved they might be." He frowned. "I'm afraid one of these days I'm going to have to try an uptown office as well as this one. I need paying patients so I can get the money to provide the medicine my unpaying patients need!" He laughed, but it wasn't a light laugh.

Suddenly Arleen clutched his arm. Across the street a half dozen boys in black leather jackets, the flamboyantly painted rooster on their backs, were lounging against the front of the building that housed the poolroom.

Arleen had noticed them because she'd had the uncanny feeling she was being watched. She'd turned her head and stared into the heavy-lidded, cruel eyes of the blond boy who had viciously ground the sparrow's legs under his heel and challenged her to do something to save the bird.

She shivered and turned quickly back to Mark. "That boy," she said, in a low, tense whisper, "the blond one with the elaborate hairdo. Who is he, Mark?"

Mark wasn't subtle about it. He turned around and stared calmly across the street, then looked back at her. "Lonnie Michos," he said. "Any particular reason you wanted to know?"

Arleen told him about the bird episode. "Rose Luigui mentioned him to Peter Rossi. She said this Lonnie called Peter a little man, not big enough to lead the Roosters. Peter told her Lonnie was a punk, and Rose said he was going to have to prove that."

Mark nodded soberly. "It will come to that," he said. He frowned. "Peter Rossi is a bitter, mixed-up, unhappy kid, but deep down inside he's not bad. It isn't the same with Lonnie Michos. Lonnie would be bad no matter what kind of home he came from, no matter how many advantages he had. He likes being cruel."

Arleen felt a coldness across her spine. She was certain Lonnie Michos' eyes were on her again. She wet her lips and touched Mark's arm.

"Let's go try a cup of Barney's coffee," she said. Her voice shook just a trifle. "Please."

Mark's eyes were focused on her lips. He lifted his head and seemed to shake himself. "Sure," he said.

CHAPTER 10

"AND BURIED in the heart, a tear."

Arleen frowned. "Now why in heaven's name would I remember that line? I can't even recall the poem it's from." She was tired, and the weariness hung from her shoulders like a mantle of despair. It had been a grueling day, beginning with finding Anna Luigui unconscious on the floor.

Five o'clock had not come a moment too soon. Miss Horne, the supervisor of nurses, had asked cheerfully when Arleen walked into the office, "And how is our angel of Leland Street this hot, dull afternoon?"

Arleen ran a hand through the hair that curled damply under her blue cap. "I don't feel like an angel," she said, with a half-hearted attempt at a smile. The despair in her voice was plainly evident.

Miss Horne frowned, her dark blue eyes searching Arleen's weary face understandingly. "You're letting conditions get you down," she told her. "You have to look past the poverty, Arleen."

Arleen said slowly, heavily, "Can they look past their own poverty, Miss Horne? Could you? Could I?"

The supervisor said quietly, "I don't know. I think I could. I think you could, too. It's been done, you know. People have looked past their poverty, intense grief, and incapacity, and won out." She sighed. "And others have lost."

Arleen said softly, "Neelie Ryan is like that. She's able to look past the bad things. Dr. Wynter said she's able to have hope when there isn't hope; see a future where there is no future."

The dark blue eyes swept across Arleen's face. The older nurse said softly, "You're very fond of him, aren't you?"

"Dr. Wynter?" Arleen asked, although she knew it was Mark Miss Horn was talking about. She flushed. "I like him, if that's what you mean. I like him as a person, and as a doctor."

The other woman said, "And not as a man, Arleen?"

Arleen's flush deepened. "I'm not in love with Dr. Wynter, Miss Horne."

The supervisor smiled. "I'm glad to hear that, Arleen. It would be very unwise for a young woman to fall in love with Dr. Wynter. I'm afraid he's much too busy being a doctor to have any of the baser urges. And heaven help a woman if he ever did get around to proposing to her. She'd starve to death!"

Arleen said, with dignity, "It's not likely that I'll fall in love with any man, Miss Horne. Love is something I'm not really interested in."

She saw the supervisor's eyes widen in startled amazement. "You're not interested in love? Oh, you poor, dear, misguided child, then you *are* a likely target. There's no victim so sure as the one who is certain she'll never be a victim."

"I was the victim once," Arleen said slowly. "I'm not interested in being one again."

"Oh," the supervisor said, in a voice suddenly fraught with understanding.

Arleen thought, fiercely, as she drove to her apartment, "I do wish people would stop warning me not to fall in love with Dr. Wynter!"

She'd hardly stepped inside the door when the phone rang.

Guy Newman's pleasant voice said cheerfully, "I hope you're hungry enough for a nice, thick steak, because that's what I have in mind for our dinner tonight. And have you missed me?"

"Yes, to both questions." Arleen laughed, surprised to find how really pleased she was to hear the sound of his voice.

"Fine," he said. "Pick you up in an hour and a half?"

"Make it two hours," Arleen said.

"It doesn't take you two hours to get beautiful," he said. "I can vouch for that."

"This particular nurse wants to lie down for a few moments before she attempts to make herself beautiful."

"Hard day?" Guy asked.

"Hard day."

Guy looked at her across one of the white-clothed tables at Roland's Steak House. Arleen was wearing a black dress with a string of artificial pearls at her throat.

He said, both his eyes and his voice intensely serious, "I was sure I remembered you exactly, but I'd forgotten how really lovely you are."

Arleen stared down at her hands, and then up at him. "You're in a very complimentary mood, Guy," she said lightly.

His eyes held hers. "I feel complimentary when I'm with you," he said. He stared at the glowing tip of the cigarette he held. "Any claims on your heart while I've been gone?"

Arleen shook her head. "No claims. I like my heart exactly the way it is, Guy. I don't want to share it with anyone."

He said carefully, "If you shared half with someone else, you'd get his half in return. It would work out mathematically sound. You'd end up with one whole heart."

Arleen said tightly, "Your logic isn't entirely sound, Guy.

Sometimes you end up not with one whole heart, but with a damaged half."

The waiter appeared with the steaks, and Arleen attacked hers with vigor. Not only because she was actually hungry, but because the appearance of the waiter gave her a chance to shift the conversation.

She looked up at Guy as she cut her steak. "I don't think I've ever been so hungry!"

"Nor so glad to see a steak."

Meeting his eyes, Arleen flushed and said, "Well, it wasn't exactly a topic of conversation I thoroughly enjoy." She took a bite of steak. "It's delicious." She sighed. "So many of my dinner dates have been with interns and young residents. You settle for hamburgers and French fries and even then, quite often you buy your own."

Guy said, grinning, "So how I really rate with you is as a date who can afford to feed you steaks."

Arleen, a bite of steak partway to her mouth, halted the fork in midair and stared at him across the table. "I was only joking," she protested. "I wasn't being serious. I thought you understood that!"

He laughed. "Go ahead and eat your steak, and don't fret. I understand a lot of things you don't think I do."

The floor show came on at ten. The young girl singer had a low, throaty voice admirably suited to the type of ballad she was singing.

Guy found Arleen's hand under the table and held it tightly. She made no attempt to withdraw it. He released her hand just before the lights went on.

Later they danced. "Moonlight and roses," Guy said, in a low voice, against her ear, as they danced. "A girl like you close to my heart. Can heaven hold more?"

Arleen was upset. "Guy," she said fiercely, "stop making love to me!"

"Making love to you?" he said. "Why, Arleen, those are the words of a song. I was only trying out my singing voice."

"I never heard that song."

"You don't get around nearly enough, then." He was tender and teasing at the same time.

Standing on the dancefloor before the next dance began, he said softly, "I had a few dates back home with a girl I've dated off and on for about a year. I've always thought she was a pretty good dancer, but this time she felt like lead in my arms. You feel like eiderdown. Everything she did I compared to you. And she lost."

Arleen shook her head. "Please, Guy, don't."

"Don't fall in love with you?" he asked her softly. "It's already happened, Arleen. I *am* in love with you. I'm only waiting for you to return my love."

"I told you I wasn't ever going to fall in love with anyone. I told you that the first time we went out together!"

"Did you? Then this is entirely my own fault, isn't it?"

Arleen said, "Love hurts. I don't want to be hurt, Guy." There was a childish tremor in her voice.

He said gently, "I wouldn't hurt you, Arleen. I want to marry you, and take care of you, and protect you."

"Please, Guy, don't propose to me!"

"I know quite a few women who would jump with joy if I ever got around to proposing to them. Back home I'm considered quite a catch."

Arleen said quickly, "I'm flattered, Guy, only. . . ."

"Only you aren't in love with me," he finished for her.

"I'm not in love with anyone," Arleen said, her calm restored.

"I've rushed you too much," Guy said. "I'll have to give you more time to get used to the idea; to get used to me."

"All of the time in the world won't change things. I don't want to love anyone, Guy, and I don't want anyone to love me. More and more I'm beginning to think I'm a dedicated nurse, as Dr. Wynter is a dedicated doctor. I can't just go home at night and dismiss these people from my mind. I can't be an eight-to-five nurse."

Guy Newman was regarding her searchingly. "Dr. Wynter," he said. "Methinks I hear the name of my rival."

Arleen felt her face redden. "I'm getting awfully tired of having people worry about my falling in love with Mark Wynter!"

"So it's Mark, is it?" Guy said. He was frowning.

Arleen said slowly, "He's a doctor with an office on Leland Street. That's in the slum area. He buys medicine out of his own pocket to treat his patients. They pay him when they can, which in most cases is never. He's a fine person and a fine doctor, but I do not love him. I am in no danger of falling in love with him. I hope you'll believe me!"

"He sounds more and more formidable. But I've licked stronger adversaries. After all, I'm a slum kid. We're born fighting."

Arleen said, in a low voice, "Let's not talk about Dr. Wynter any more, Guy. Let's not talk about anything personal."

He looked down at her, his lips twisted in a wry smile. "All right," he said, "it's a deal."

They finished the dance and went back to their table. Arleen said, with determined lightness, "I suppose you drove to see the mission at Capistrano, and the swallows."

To her suprise, he nodded. "It's really a most peaceful place. I hadn't imagined. . . ."

Arleen said, "I have a patient who's bedridden with arthritis. The dream of her life, what she's got left of it, is to go to Capistrano. She wants to see the swallows when they come back. She can't imagine anything more wonderful than that."

"Everybody in the slums has a dream, of one kind or another. Mostly it's to escape."

Arleen said, a shaky edge to her voice, "Neelie thinks every one of us has a big chunk of happiness coming to him; that God made things that way. For her chunk she wants to see Capistrano and the swallows. For her husband Al's chunk, she wants a chance for him to be able to grow flowers all year long."

Guy said slowly, "It doesn't sound impossible. It's not as if she asked for a million dollars."

"She might as well have asked for it. They're on relief. Her husband's over sixty. He's fundamentally a good man, but he's a weak one. Whenever he gets a few dimes he buys himself a bottle of wine, so that he can forget he's a failure."

Guy asked, "Doesn't he work?"

"He's tried to find work," Arleen said, "but he's told he's too old. It's morale breaking."

Guy said slowly, "Hugging other people's misery to you isn't going to change things for them. It isn't going to make it either better or worse."

"I'd like Neelie to get that chunk of happiness she's so convinced she's going to have one day. I'd like to go to her, carrying it on a silver platter. I'd like to say to her, 'Here it is, Neelie. Here's your dream.'" Her voice broke.

Guy stood up abruptly. "I'm taking you home," he said.

In the car, he drew her to him. "When I was a kid in the slums," he said, "I had two dreams—to make a lot of money so I could lift myself out of the slums. And to marry a girl, who, surprisingly, looked and thought and acted almost exactly like you."

Arleen said, in a low voice, "We weren't going to talk about it any more tonight."

Outside her door, he cupped her chin in his hand and

kissed her. "Don't tell me not to fall in love with you," he said, "because I'm already in love. And I'm not at all floored by your telling me you're never going to fall in love with anyone. As I told you, I'm a guy who likes to butt his head against stone walls, seeing whether he can effect a breakthrough."

He pulled Arleen's head down and kissed her on the forehead. "Pick you up tomorrow night about nine-thirty," he said. "I have to go to Detroit and I may be a bit late getting back." When Arleen opened her mouth to protest, he said, "You know you promised me all your evenings while I was in town."

Arleen shook her head. "Guy—"

"About nine," he said.

"Guy—"

But, grinning, he turned and waved to her from the outside door, then closed it after him. She thought he'd gone, but he opened the door again and said, "And wear that red thing you wore the first night I met you."

Arleen sighed, opened the door and went into the apartment. She was surprised to find Evelyn at home. "Charley had to work," Evelyn said. "Again!" She frowned, and added with a trace of petulance, "I almost went out with that cute intern at the hospital." She swung off the chair. "Hey, know who called you tonight?"

"Who?" Arleen asked, with no real interest. She was still distressed over Guy's declaration.

"A Dr. Mark Wynter," Evelyn said, and watched Arleen's face avidly for her reaction.

CHAPTER 11

ARLEEN'S HEART gave a jerk. Her eyes widened. "Mark called?" She felt flustered. "Why would he call me?"

Evelyn shrugged.

"Didn't he say what he wanted?" Arleen persisted.

"When I told him you were out on a date," Evelyn said, "he hung up." Her blue eyes regarded Arleen with amused shrewdness. "You don't suppose he was jealous, do you? The unattainable Dr. Wynter?"

"Oh, don't be silly!" Arleen flung at her. "Do you think

I should phone him? Maybe the call had something to do with Neelie Ryan."

Evelyn said, "Phone him at this hour of the night? He's probably deep in his beauty sleep."

Arleen frowned. "It could be something serious. I could be needed. . . ."

"Oh, go on and phone him, honey," Evelyn told her. "You're going to, no matter what I say." She studied Arleen intently. "I'm going to give this advice to you, gratis. Don't bring your job home with you. You can't be a nurse every waking hour. Throw off your job when you throw off your uniform. That's darn good advice, honey, and you'd do well to heed it."

Arleen sighed. "I wish it were as easy as that, Evelyn."

Evelyn said slowly, "I achieved it. I had to. In the beginning I cried over every patient. It broke my heart when I had to watch them die. Then I developed a kind of callousness. Otherwise I couldn't have gone on being a nurse."

"There's that word callous again," Arleen thought. She shook her head at Evelyn. "I know," she said. "I'll try."

She looked at the telephone; hesitated, then looked up Mark's number and dialed him. The phone rang for a long time. She was on the point of hanging up when his voice, thick with sleep, answered.

Arleen felt a moment of panic. It had been a crazy idea to phone him. What was she going to say? If it had been important, he'd have told Evelyn to have her call him back.

She swallowed. "This is Miss Anderson." She gave a nervous laugh. "Arleen for short. My roommate said you called while I was out, and I thought it might be something important. I'm sorry I woke you up. I did wake you up, didn't I?"

His voice sounded crisp, in spite of the sleepiness. He said, "You're taking your work much too seriously. Did you really think I'd phone you to come and take care of one of my patients? At night? In this area?"

"I'm sorry," Arleen said, unhappily.

He went on as if she had not interrupted him. "I merely phoned to see if you'd like to go to a movie. I noticed a Western was playing again, and it occurred to me that you might like to see it."

"I'm sorry," Arleen said again. "I'd have liked to see it, Mark."

He said, "Don't be. It wasn't worth being sorry about. It was horrible."

Arleen waited, but he did not say, "The next time there's

67

a Western playing, perhaps you'd like to see it with me."
Instead, he stifled a yawn. "Now, if you'll just allow me to go back to sleep—"

"Oh. Oh yes, of course," Arleen said, quickly, and hung up. Her cheeks were burning when she turned from the phone. He'd had no reason to act so rude. She'd only been trying to be nice!

Evelyn flashed her a quick look, but made no comment.

Arleen undressed, washed, went through her usual nightly routine. But when she got into bed she found herself unable to sleep. She lay for a few moments staring up at the ceiling, and then she decided to get up and write her mother a letter. She owed her one.

She got up and slipped into a faded cotton robe. It was one she'd had for years and years. Her mother had protested when she had packed it, "Arleen, dear, it's positively disreputable!"

"But I like it," Arleen had told her cheerfully. "It's comfortable, the most comfortable robe I've ever had."

Her father had sided with her. "If a gal can't be comfortable when she's alone, when can she be?" He'd kissed her. "Your mother feels the same way about my old fishing hat. I have to hide it from her or she'd give it away."

Her mother had laughed ruefully. "Who'd take it?"

Tears stung Arleen's eyes as she got out pen and paper, sat down at the desk in the living room and began composing the letter in her mind.

Pen poised above the paper, she stared unseeingly at the blank page. Back home when she'd be confused and unhappy and beset with problems, her mother would say cheerfully, "Here now, let's sit down and talk this out, and I'm sure we can come up with a way out."

Arleen clutched the pen tighter. "Dear Mother," she wanted to write, "I'm so mixed up and unhappy. I know I shouldn't carry my job around with me, but I can't seem to help it. It's poor Neelie Ryan and the Luiguis, and the boy who crushed the sparrow just to see how I'd take it, and Peter Rossi, who wanted to go to high school and couldn't make it. It's them, and it's this young man who swears he's in love with me. I don't want him to be in love with me! But sometimes, like right now, I think about being married to someone like him—someone I don't love—and how safe and secure it would be. A nice, neat package all tied up."

She blinked back the tears, and her mind continued with

68

the phrasing of the letter. "It would be wrong to marry a man when you don't love him; when you know you'll never love him." She blinked again. "The thing is, I'm afraid. Oh, not of physical things . . . not of Leland Street or the people there. What I'm afraid of is that my heart isn't so secure as I thought it was! I'm afraid that maybe I *can* fall in love. Oh, Mother, I'm afraid that perhaps I've already fallen in love! And he's not the kind of man to fall in love with, any more than Johnny was!"

She drew an unsteady breath and began writing the letter, but it wasn't at all what she had composed in her mind. It was a rambling, cheerful, affectionate letter, with no word of her unhappiness in it.

"I'm coming home on my vacation," she wrote. "I wish it could be during the haying season, but I know it won't be. Does the hay smell as sweet, when it's cut, as it used to? Remember how I used to drive out into the country so I could smell it at closer range?"

She signed the letter, "Your adoring daughter," folded it and put it in an envelope, addressed and stamped it, and put it out in plain sight so she wouldn't forget to mail it in the morning.

"If I don't fall asleep now," she told herself, "I'll have to prescribe a sleeping tablet. And since I never take sleeping tablets, I shall have to go to sleep."

She lay, her eyes closed, forcing herself to count sheep. "One sheep, two sheep, three sheep. Oh, there's a little black lamb—five sheep, six, seven." Her mind began to wander. "Now, why would I think I was falling in love with Mark Wynter? That would be a crazy thing to do. It's just that people are forever warning me against falling in love with him. I've taken it to heart. It's becoming a psychological thing with me."

Determinedly she brought her mind back to her sheep counting. "Eight, nine, ten." She opened her eyes for a second. On top of everything else, Mark Wynter was rude. One of the rudest men she'd ever met, she told herself firmly.

"Eleven, twelve."

Evelyn said, "For pete's sake, Arleen, what are you doing in there? If you're talking in your sleep, talk louder so I can hear what you're saying. That mumbling you're doing is very frustrating."

Arleen said, "I'm not talking in my sleep. I'm counting sheep."

The entire city seemed enclosed in a haze of heat as Arleen left the tenement building where Neelie Ryan and the Luiguis lived.

It was after two. She'd had other calls to make in the area, and she had a new patient in the building—the woman on the top floor whom Mark had been hurrying to see the first time Arleen had met him.

Mrs. Murphy was garrulous, filled with self-pity, a neurotic, but she did have a very real heart condition.

She wasn't bedridden, but she was lonely. Usually she had a long list of symptoms with which to regale Arleen the moment she stepped inside the door.

Arleen felt sorry for her. It was sad to be old, sick, and terribly alone. But the woman had a small pension that provided for a window fan and other small luxuries that kept her fairly comfortable.

Arleen had looked in on the Luigui baby and was happily surprised to find Carmella reasonably clean, only slightly wet, and fed.

"Well," she said cheerfully, after she had weighed Carmella, "she's gaining fine now." She laid the baby down and looked at Pietro, who was standing against the kitchen wall watching her with wary eyes.

"Is Pietro still getting his vitamins, Mrs. Luigui?" she asked Anna, and, at the woman's surly nod, "Is he taking them?"

"Sure," Anna said. "Sure he takes them." She didn't look at Arleen.

Arleen said sternly, "They aren't candy to be fought over, Mrs. Luigui. They are vitamins prescribed especially for Pietro to cure his skin condition. I don't think the doctor would like it if he thought Pietro weren't getting the medicine he prescribed for him."

Anna said sullenly, "He get them. Who said he no get them, huh?"

"I only wanted to make sure, Mrs. Luigui. You see, when the doctor examines Pietro he'll be able to tell whether or not Pietro has been taking his vitamins regularly."

Out on the street, Arleen thought wryly, "I'm taking a page from Mark's book. I'm using a bluff." She wiped her forehead with a clean tissue. "I'm learning," she thought. "I'm learning how to deal with these people."

She stood for a moment, breathing in the hot air. The heat had been building up all day. It was bound to rain soon. She was glad Neelie had the fan. It gave Arleen a sense of well-being to think about it.

70

She looked at the street. Always, it seemed, when she came here, she had to look at the street. Paper and refuse crowded against the gutters. The stench of garbage from the overloaded cans in front of the buildings assailed her nostrils. She thought of the sweet smell of hay in the country, and how these people had never, and would never, know such a smell.

The knowledge saddened her, and she thought, "I must remember what Mark said. I can only do my job; I cannot change their way of life."

Across the street was one of the innumerable peddler's carts. A group of women were haggling over some merchandise. There was also a barbershop, a grocery store, an empty store window, and the poolhall.

Arleen always looked last at the poolhall, fearing to feel Lonnie Michos' heavy-lidded, cruel gaze.

He hadn't bothered her since the afternoon of the bird episode, but she would sometimes have the craziest feeling, as she walked to her car or sat in it for a moment before turning on the ignition, that he was watching her.

Her hands would tremble, and coldness would ride up and down her spine. She hadn't mentioned the feeling to anyone, and she had tried to laugh herself out of it. So far she hadn't succeeded.

She began walking to her car. A truck had been parked in her usual place and she'd had to park nearly a block from the tenement building.

"That's what I get for being late this afternoon," she told herself. As she walked, she thought she detected a faint breeze beginning to stir. A good, stiff breeze would surely indicate rain, and the cooling would begin.

Her forehead was once again beaded with perspiration. She delved into her purse for a handkerchief. When she lifted her head she looked into the narrow, gloating eyes of Lonnie Michos.

His blond hair was arranged in meticulous waves, one lock jutting forward like a rooster's tail. A dirty T-shirt covered his thin, sloping shoulders and bony chest.

Behind him were a half dozen other boys in similar dress. It was the first time Arleen had ever seen them minus the familiar black leather jackets.

She thought, with a touch of hysteria, "It must not really be as hot as I think it is!" Her common sense told her that the very worst thing she could do would be to show fear, so she kept her chin high and forced herself to survey them calmly.

"You seem to be blocking my way, boys. I have other calls to make. Would you mind letting me by?"

"Would we mind letting her by?" Lonnie gave a shrill giggle and looked at the others. "Whata you think? We mind?"

Arleen saw they had encircled her. She felt the dryness of fear tighten her throat. "Mark will come along," she assured herself. "Mark will know how to deal with them. I don't have to be afraid." But a shiver of fear shook her.

"What do you want?" she asked, trying to fasten her gaze on all of them at once. "If you'll just tell me. . . ."

Lonnie gave that high giggle again. "Why, doll," he said, "we just want to talk to you, that's all. Someplace private like. We got a lot to say to you, ain't we, boys?"

The others were silent, except for a snicker that shook the group.

Arleen said, with all the dignity she could muster, "My name is not 'doll,' it's Miss Anderson. And when you're speaking to me, I want you to call me that!"

"Okay, doll," Lonnie said. He reached out a hand to touch her.

A voice said sharply, "Let her alone!"

It wasn't Mark Wynter who stood there, Arleen saw. It was young Peter Rossi.

CHAPTER 12

"OH, WE wasn't figuring on harming her," Lonnie Michos said. "We was just wanting to talk to her, wasn't we, boys?" His high giggle sounded as he turned to look at the others for confirmation.

There was a tense silence, as if the other boys were merely spectators, warily deciding on which side to embrace.

Peter surveyed the group with scorn. "Since when have the Roosters become women attackers?" His lips curled. "Any low punk can maul a woman. I thought the Roosters had brains!" He directed a sneering glance at Lonnie Michos. "This your idea, Lonnie? A guy who curls his hair *could* come up with a crazy idea like this!"

"Lay off me!" Lonnie Michos snarled.

Peter said coldly, "Miss Anderson is a nurse. Nurses and doctors are supposed to have free access to anyplace on Leland Street. Like the military in East Berlin."

"This ain't East Berlin," Lonnie said. He giggled again. "And who made that rule, huh?"

"Nobody made it," Peter said. "It just is, that's all."

He walked over and put a hand on Arleen's elbow. She hoped she looked calmer than she felt, as Peter edged their way through the circle that fell back at their approach.

"Where's your car?" Peter asked.

Arleen pointed it out. She said shakily, "Would they have let me go if you hadn't come along?"

"I don't know," he said. There was antagonism in his glance. "How come you've always got to be around, messing things up for me?"

Arleen said softly, "Peter, I don't know how to thank you."

"Break it off," he told her curtly. "I got some thinking to do. I've got to go back there and straighten them out."

Arleen said, "Peter, will you get into trouble? Dr. Wynter said this Lonnie Michos was a really bad boy, not like you, but really bad."

Peter scowled at her. "Don't go fretting over me," he told her. "I don't need anybody to worry about me. I can take care of myself. And I can take care of Lonnie Michos, if I have to."

Arleen watched him as he swaggered off, his steps slow and deliberate, his thumbs hooked in the loops of his blue jeans. "The hero in a second-rate Western, striding down the street to face the big, bad gunman," she thought, and wanted to laugh. But she knew it was far from funny. These weren't kids playing a game. They played for real.

Because she was deeply concerned about Peter, she felt the need to see Mark Wynter. Driving to his office, she found she was trembling violently. It was the reaction, she knew, to the fear she had tried not to show in front of the gang.

Mark's office was in a dilapidated frame building, and the sign out front was as worn as the building itself. Mark Wynter, MD. The letters sprawled across the board, uneven, out of proportion.

Arleen opened the door and walked inside. It was the first time she'd been to Mark's office. There was a small narrow room, obviously the waiting room. It held a wooden bench and two straight-backed chairs. A bent old lady, terribly thin, was sitting on the bench. She glanced up briefly when Arleen came in, then stared down at her clasped hands again.

The door into the other room opened and Mark looked out. His eyes widened when he saw Arleen. He said, "Be with you presently," his voice crisp.

He glanced at the thin old woman and his voice gentled. "Come on in, Maggie, and we'll have a look at you."

Arleen selected one of the chairs and sat down. She looked at the peeling wallpaper with careful concentration.

Would the boys have let her go if Peter hadn't come along? And why had Peter helped her? There had been nothing to require him to help her—nothing except, possibly, his own code of ethics. Fundamentally Peter Rossi did not belong to the world of street gangs and crime.

The wallpaper had once been an ugly brown with green leaves trailing in a haphazard pattern through it. Why would anyone select such ugly paper?

She stared down at her hands, clasped in her lap just as the older woman's hands had been clasped. How many boys like Peter Rossi were there? Boys who were fundamentally good, but who would continue in the world of street gangs and crime, because there was no other way for them to find an identity?

And what was happening to Peter? Did a gang take revenge, even on their leader, if they did not like something he did?

Arleen knew nothing of street gangs. Before her work had taken her into Leland Street, her closest association with them had been from newspaper headlines when something they did was violent enough to bring a riot squad.

Sunlight filtered in through the not too clean window panes of the one large window the room boasted. She was carefully surveying the window, but not really seeing it, when Mark came out of the other room.

She heard the sound of the door opening and turned her head. Mark had one arm loosely around the woman's shoulders. "You be sure and take those pills exactly as I told you," he warned her. "I don't want to hear of you neglecting it." He gave her a mock scowl.

She looked up at him. "What if I don't eat a meal, Doctor. Should I take them anyway, just like I had et?"

Mark nodded. His hand squeezed her shoulders. "Your appetite will improve after the pills begin working," he told

74

her. "A few weeks on those pills, Maggie, and I'll probably have to put you on a reducing diet."

She gave a thin, high laugh. "I ain't been fat a day in my life, Doctor!"

He grinned at her. "Now you're bragging." He took his arm from around her shoulder. "I want to see you again in a week, Maggie; sooner than that if the pills don't work the way I told you they would."

There was adulation on her face. "You always help me when I come here, Doctor." She fumbled with a shabby pocketbook. "As soon as my pension comes, I'll pay you a bit of something on my bill. It's just. . . ."

Mark smiled at her, cutting off the flow of embarrassed explanations. "What would I do with money, Maggie? You sick people keep me so darn busy I never have time to go anyplace. Where would I spend it? I'd end up by hoarding it, and you know what they call hoarders—misers. You wouldn't want me to become a miser, would you?"

Her face seemed to break. "You're a good man, Doctor," she said. "The Lord'll reward you for how kind you are to everyone."

"Now, Maggie," he teased her, "you know I'm not always so kind! You go along home now, take one of those pills, and go to bed for a couple of hours. It'll do you good."

He walked her to the door, closed it after her. When he turned around, Arleen was stunned by the despair that looked at her out of his eyes.

"She has terminal cancer," he said. "I give her pain pills. They help a little. I kid her that she never ate right, and now she has stomach trouble, the result of too many pastries and hot fudge sundaes when she was a girl. She doesn't know she has cancer. Maybe I should tell her, but I'm not going to.

"Toward the end, when the pain gets too bad, I'm going to have to find a place for her in the hospital. There's no help for her. The cancer had progressed too far when she came to me."

His eyes hardened; became angry. "Aren't you going to tell me there's still a chance of a miracle?"

Arleen didn't answer him. He frowned, and stared at her, as if really seeing her for the first time. "Surely you aren't here as a patient?"

"No," Arleen said. She stared at him, the events which had brought her to his office crowded from her mind. "Mark, I'm sorry. I wish there were something. . . ."

He said curtly, "There's nothing. And I don't like maudlin-ness. Let's not talk about my patient. Let's talk about you and what brought you here."

Arleen felt her face redden. Was this the man whose hands had pressed into her shoulders; who had touched her lips for a brief second with tender passion? Whose voice had been gentleness itself as he'd talked to his cancer patient?

She said unsteadily, "It's Peter Rossi, Mark." As briefly as possible, she told him what had happened. "Will they do anything to him, Mark, because he helped me?" She regarded the frowning Mark anxiously.

He said, "As long as Peter can control them, he'll be their leader. But the minute he can no longer control them, they'll be on him like a wolf pack."

Arleen shivered. "That boy—that Lonnie Michos—Mark, the way he looked at Peter! It was the same look he had when he crushed the bird under his heel. He didn't mean for the bird to die, he wanted it to lie there and suffer. And he wanted to see what effect that would have on me, what I'd do about it!"

Mark's lips tightened. "That Lonnie Michos enjoys being cruel."

"You've got to stop him, then," Arleen said. "There's no telling what he might be planning to do to Peter."

"Wait here," Mark told her. "I won't be gone long."

He had hardly left the office when a young girl carrying a baby entered. She was very pretty, Arleen thought, and she could have been no more than fifteen. She felt a tug at her heart, and smiled at the girl.

"That's a very pretty baby."

The girl shrugged. "Yes, ma'am." She seemed to have no desire to talk.

Arleen was standing up staring out the window when Mark returned. He glanced at the young girl. "Be right with you, Lori," he said.

He took Arleen by one arm, walked her to the door, and told her in a low voice, "Peter still leads the Roosters. From what I hear, he gave them quite a long talk." His lips quirked. "How much of what he said got through to them, I couldn't say."

He led her out onto the street. They stood for a moment under the hot sun, beside Arleen's car. "Perhaps you'd better ask for a reassignment," he said. "Word is around that Lonnie Michos plans to take over the Roosters. And some of them are siding with him. A gang thrives on excitement, and Lonnie promises them more excitement than Peter does."

Arleen shook her head. Her small chin was held high; her lips were tight. "I'm a nurse, Mark. This is my district. Do you think I'd desert Neelie Ryan and the other people who need me, because I let myself be frightened by a few teenage boys?"

Mark warned, "Don't underestimate these kids. They can be vicious." He sighed. "I guess I knew you wouldn't take my advice and go find a safe place in which to practise nursing."

Arleen flushed with anger. She said coldly, "Don't make it sound as if I'm a child playing a game, Mark!"

His eyes narrowed. "Why don't you get married?" he asked her. "I'm sure you've had plenty of chances. It takes a strong, tough woman to do a visiting nurse's job."

Arleen said tightly, "I haven't heard any complaints about my work from the people I take care of. And if I'm not quite strong enough, or tough enough, as yet, I can learn." Her chin went an inch higher. "I can become callous too, in time, if it becomes necessary!"

Mark's gray eyes swept her face; warmed. Without a word, he opened the car door for her. "I'd better get back to my patient," he said.

Arleen was trembling when she pulled away from the curb. But it was a quiver of anger this time, not of fear.

She was surprised to receive a phone call from Guy Newman that night. Evelyn was on night duty at the hospital and Arleen was stretched out on the sofa, trying to concentrate on a magazine story, when the phone rang.

She had just about decided to set the alarm for eight-thirty and take a nap. An hour would be more than enough time to get ready for her date with Guy. She wasn't looking forward to the date with any real pleasure, even though she enjoyed Guy's company. She knew, almost with certainty, that he would bring up personal things again tonight.

And she did not want to become involved in a sparring session once again. She was not in love with Guy Newman. She did not want to be in love with him. Her lips thinned. She denied the sudden pounding of her heart. She did not want to be in love with anyone. And she was not. She was only in love with her job.

She lifted the phone when it rang, letting the magazine

she'd been reading fall shut. It didn't matter. She'd lost interest in the story anyway.

"I'm going to have to break our date," Guy said. He sounded hurried and harassed. "I have to fly back home. I'm at the airport now, waiting for my plane to take off. Something has come up. If I fail to find the answer, my company stands to lose a half-million-dollar contract." His voice hardened. "I'll find the answer."

Arleen said quietly, "I'm sure you will, Guy. I'll be keeping my fingers crossed."

"It will take me a week, ten days, maybe two weeks, but when I come back, our date still goes."

"Yes," Arleen said.

His voice lowered. "And I want you to think about what I asked you. And give me an answer when I come back."

"Guy, it's no good," Arleen said, distressed. "I can't. . . . You mustn't. . . ."

He cut in on her words. "I'm really a very nice person," he told her. "I promise not to beat you. Or make you milk cows. Or bring me my breakfast in bed. None of those things."

"I'm not the marrying kind," Arleen said.

"Think about it," he told her. "Think about all of the advantages you'll have, being Mrs. Guy Newman, wife of the rising young businessman. And on top of all that, I love you." He hung up.

Arleen found she wanted to weep as she hung up the phone. "He can't be in love with me," she told herself frantically. "There hasn't been time. He hardly knows me!"

How long had it taken her to fall in love with Johnny? A week? She'd been head over heels in a week.

She was startled, the next time she went to Leland Street, to be accosted by Rose Luigui.

Rose faced her angrily. "Why did you get Peter in trouble? Huh, nurse lady?"

Arleen shook her head. "Trouble?"

Rose practically spit the words at her. "You made him help you. And now Lonnie is saying that next time Peter'll turn cop, maybe! Lonnie's got it in for him because of you!"

Arleen said quietly, "You know that isn't true. And I didn't make Peter do anything. He did it on his own, because he isn't really the kind of boy he tries to make out he is."

"You let him alone!" Rose said. "He doesn't need you!"

Arleen said slowly, watching the girl, "I didn't know Peter Rossi was so important to you, Rose." She frowned, then

78

smiled. "He's not like the others in the gang. Peter could do something with his life. Maybe you could help him, Rose. Maybe the two of you. . . ."

Rose's eyes darkened. "You can just plain go to hell with that kind of talk!" she flung at Arleen, and ran from her.

CHAPTER 13

SHE FOUND Neelie Ryan poring over a pile of magazines on her bed. Al was asleep in a chair by the one window, his head flung back. He was snoring loudly. Arleen thought how pathetic he looked when asleep, all of the defiance gone from him, just a tired old man.

She recalled what Mark had said . . . that if ever Al fell down he couldn't get up. Neelie would get up and go on, but not Al.

He mustn't fall down! She turned her attention to Neelie. "Well, it looks as if someone dropped a carload of magazines on your bed."

Neelie nodded happily. "Miss Gibbons brought them to me; said she'd read them and didn't know what on earth to do with them." And at Arleen's amazed look, she said, nodding as if in agreement with herself, "Oh, Miss Gibbons ain't near so hard as she lets on to be. Why, I wouldn't be surprised if she had a real kind heart under that mean way of hers."

Arleen said, half to herself, "I wouldn't be surprised, either." Miss Gibbons had been a long time in social work. Evidently she'd learned, the way Evelyn had learned in her nursing job, that she had to become just a bit calloused around the edges if she were going to go on working.

She piled the magazines at the foot of the bed, got a washbasin, filled it with water, laid out soap, towels, and alcohol, feeling almost as much familiarity with her surroundings as if she were in her own home.

Neelie said, admiringly, "My, Miss Anderson, but you work so quick. I never saw nobody move so fast as you do. It ain't much wonder you're so skinny."

Arleen grinned at her as she began sponging the thin body. "Who's calling who skinny? I guess you rate as the fat woman of the circus?"

"Oh, I used to have some fat on me when I was younger,"

79

Neelie said. "I always worked hard, but then I ate hard, too."

Arleen combed Neelie's gray hair back off her face in a more cooling style. She said, "You're lucky, Neelie, to have natural curly hair; the wetter it gets, the more it curls."

Neelie nodded. "It's saved me a whole lot of money I'd have spent on permanents," she said.

When Arleen had finished repacking her bag, she saw that Al was awake. She frowned, hesitated, and then said, "Al, you get around. Tell me, are Rose Luigui and Peter Rossi . . . are they . . . is he. . . ."

Neelie said, "She wants to know if they're in love, Al."

The old man shrugged. He said levelly, "Why don't you ask one of them, Miss Anderson?"

Arleen flushed. She said, in a low voice, "I tried to ask Rose." She sighed. "They're both such bitter youngsters, that I thought . . . well, I thought if they were friends, maybe each of them could help the other to do something with their lives."

Al said harshly, "You talking about some miracle happening, Miss Anderson? You a miracle looker, like Dr. Wynter? Well, one ain't gonna happen. Not on Leland Street it ain't. When God goes looking for someplace to drop a miracle, He looks right past Leland Street."

Arleen could have told him that Mark Wynter no longer believed in miracles. If he ever had believed in them.

"Now, Al," Neelie chided him, "probably miracles happen around here all the time, and we don't even hear about them."

"Like what?" Al asked harshly.

"Well," Neelie said, "like maybe that little Luigui boy running out into the street and not hardly getting scratched by that car."

Al gave a hard laugh. "The guy had good brakes," he said, "and he probably wasn't driving very fast."

"All right," Neelie said cheerfully, "maybe you'll get the chance to see a real, live miracle with your very own eyes, and then I'll bet you'll think different about it." She turned her eyes on Arleen.

"Don't pay any attention to Al," she said. "Maybe them two, Rose and Peter, will fall in love with each other. And there's no one in this whole world who can say love can't do just about anything."

She looked at her husband and he looked back at her, mutely, his face twisted. "Now you take you and me, Al. If anything was to happen so's you'd need me to take care of you, why I'd be able to get right up out of this bed and do it."

Al Ryan shook his head. "Neelie, Neelie," he said.

He glanced at Arleen, hesitated, and then said slowly, "That Lonnie Michos, he's bad. He's real bad." He swallowed, and went on relentlessly, as if it were a job he did not relish, "I got a pretty good suspicion he's using marijuana—not only him, but others in the Roosters, too. It ain't far from that to heroin."

Neelie said from the bed, "Oh my, Al, you shouldn't say a thing like that unless you know it's true."

Al looked at Arleen from weary, frightened eyes. "I know it's true," he told her. "Peter's against the gang having anything to do with dope. Everybody on the street knows that. But they're operating on the sly, without him."

Arleen's heart was pounding. She opened her mouth to say something, and Al said, his voice shaking, "I should have let it go. I shouldn't have said nothing to you. I should have kept my nose out of it! If you say anything to anybody about what I told you—" he shook his head—"they'd get me." His glance slanted to Neelie, who was staring at him with sudden fright. "They'd get Neelie, too."

Arleen said, "I won't say anything, Al. Not to anyone."

His lips drew in. He said, "I've got to believe you."

Neelie said, "Al, you can trust Miss Anderson. She wouldn't tell nobody." She frowned. "A body shouldn't have to be scared of doing the right thing."

Arleen thought, "She's right. It shouldn't be this way, where the only right thing is to keep your mouth shut, no matter what goes on."

She walked down to her car, got in and turned the key in the switch. Out of the corner of an eye she saw some of the Roosters convened in front of the poolhall on the opposite side of the street, but she was not accosted.

The threatened rain of the day before had not materialized and the heat lay in shimmering waves on the sidewalk. She couldn't put what Al Ryan had told her out of her mind. What was it he had said? "It's not far from marijuana to heroin." A doctor would keep narcotics in his office. Mark would keep narcotics in his office.

Had Al heard something? Had he given her a warning for Mark? She shook her head. The heat poured like melted syrup through the open windows of the car.

No one on Leland Street would harm Mark or rifle his office. He'd kept an office there for a long time; he lived there.

No one had attempted to harm him. She'd been told that Dr. Wynter was one of the few who could walk Leland Street unaccosted, no matter how late at night it was, no matter how dark it was. He could leave his doors unlocked and no one would steal from him.

But that was before Lonnie Michos had begun to take over the Roosters, wasn't it? That was when Peter Rossi's had been the controlling hand!

A new kind of fear shook her. Fear for Mark.

It was Evelyn's turn to prepare dinner that week. She'd fixed grilled pork chops, a green salad, strawberries with rich cream. "Exactly what we need for our figures," she'd tossed humorously at Arleen across the table. And then frowned, as she saw that Arleen had hardly touched her food.

"Hey," she said, "I'm insulted. I thought I did a superb job of cooking tonight. I rate myself high in culinary skill."

Arleen said miserably, "It's not the food, Evelyn; the food is very good. It's me. I've got things on my mind."

Evelyn said, "Tell mama?"

Arleen shook her head. "I can't," she said. "I can't tell anyone." Her lips shook.

Evelyn frowned. "I have a date with Charley tonight, but I could break it. Would it help any if I stayed at home and kept you company?"

"No," Arleen said. "But thanks, Evelyn."

She paced the floor after Evelyn and her date had left. She'd promised Al she would tell no one. But did no one include Mark, who might be the victim of a contemplated crime?

At last she made up her mind. Mark needed to be told. For all she knew, perhaps Al had meant Mark to know.

She dialed Mark's number. No one answered. She hung up, and thought fiercely, "That's always the way it is. You make up your mind to do something and then you get a busy signal, or else no one answers!"

She tried again in a half hour. In another half hour. It was ten-thirty before she finally reached Mark. She said, tension sharpening her voice, "Where have you been? I've been trying to reach you for hours!"

Mark sounded surprised at the tone of her voice. "Was I supposed to be close to the telephone whenever you felt the desire to phone me?"

Arleen flushed. She said, embarrassed, "I'm sorry, Mark, it's just that I. . . ."

He said curtly, "Mrs. Murphy died. I was with her."

"Mrs. Murphy?" Arleen said. "The woman who lives in Neelie Ryan's building?"

"The same," Mark said. "Now, if you've been trying to get hold of me for hours, why don't you. . . ."

Arleen said, "Was she scared? Oh, I hope she wasn't scared."

"She was unconscious," Mark said. "She didn't know when it came."

"Oh," Arleen said, "I'm so glad. She was such a lonely thing, and I'm sure she was scared. All the time I think she was scared."

Mark sounded as if he were holding in his impatience with an effort. "Is it too much to ask why you've been trying to reach me? Surely not to make small talk at ten-thirty at night."

Arleen said, "I'm sorry." She thought, "It seems to me that I'm forever saying 'I'm sorry' about something or other to Mark!"

"I have something I must talk over with you," she told him. "It's deadly serious, Mark. I wanted to make certain you were in before I came. I'll drive right over."

"Now?" he asked, as if she'd mentioned flying to the moon at that exact moment. "At ten-thirty at night? You're driving to Leland Street?" His voice hardened. "Don't be an utter idiot! I thought you had more sense than that! Can't your talk wait until morning?"

"No," Arleen told him.

He said quietly, "Where are you?" And when she told him, he said, "I'll be right over."

Arleen said, "But you don't have a car!"

He said, "I'll find a cab."

Arleen protested, "They're terribly expensive!"

"Didn't you way it was serious?"

"Yes," Arleen said. "It's serious, Mark."

"Very well then," he said, and hung up.

He sat on the sofa in Arleen's living room, holding a cup of coffee in his two big hands. He was staring at the rug, frowning intently.

"Al Ryan's a careful man," he said. "He wouldn't tell you a thing like that unless he knew what he was talking about."

Arleen said slowly, "He told Neelie he knew it to be the

truth." Her voice trembled. "Will they find out that Al knows, Mark? Will they do something to him because he knows?"

Mark was staring at her as if he were unaware of her presence. "If those kids get to monkeying around with narcotics," he said, "we're going to have trouble on our hands." He sighed. "Peter Rossi has led the Roosters as if they were an army and he was the general. He's kept them comparatively clean, for a street gang. They've had bangs, but they've never been in any official trouble. Not one of them has a court record. But all that's going to change if Lonnie Michos takes over the Roosters. And if what Al told you is true, he's already begun taking them over."

Mark sat down his coffee cup and rose to his feet. "We can't settle it tonight," he said. He shook her gently. "Stop looking so scared."

Arleen asked, "Mark, do you keep narcotics at the office?"

"Sometimes," he said. He shook her again, his hands tightening on her shoulders. "Stop worrying," he said. "I can take care of myself. And don't lose any sleep over this. I'll think of something."

Arleen had trouble holding back the tears. Her voice shook. "Will you, Mark?"

"Of course I will," he promised, and he sounded so sure and confident that Arleen felt a brief lessening of the tension that gripped her.

He leaned toward her, hesitated, then dropped a swift kiss on the tip of her nose. He said, his voice husky, "You take everything too much to heart."

CHAPTER 14

IT WAS Miss Gibbons who told Arleen, caustically, that she should stick to being a nurse, which she was trained for, and stop trying to be a social service worker.

The day was warm and Miss Gibbons looked hot and irritable. "It's wrong for you to encourage Mrs. Ryan in her daydreams," she told Arleen. "It's best that these people learn acceptance."

Arleen said softly, "Neelie has acceptance, Miss Gibbons. She doesn't have defeat. Is that what you're suggesting she should have? Lack of hope?"

Miss Gibbons looked even more irritable. "Nonsense!" she said sharply. "All I'm saying is that these people must be helped to accept reality."

Squaring her thin shoulders, she walked away from Arleen with militarylike precision.

Arleen desperately wanted to ask Mark about the Roosters . . . Peter Rossi . . . Lonnie Michos. But Mark seemed to be deliberately avoiding her since the night she had confided in him. She wondered unhappily if he had decided she had built the whole up out of her own mind. Did he think, as did Miss Gibbons, that Arleen was invading an area for which she had no training?

Because of the feeling of panic in her, that almost amounted to desperation, she even went twice to Mark's office to see him. And found him out both times.

On her visits to Neelie, if Al were in the room, he'd go out and not return until time for Arleen to leave. If she attempted to broach the subject of Lonnie Michos or Peter Rossi to Neelie, the woman would gently but firmly change the subject.

It was as if both Al and Neelie were pretending the subject had never been brought up between them, and so consequently there was nothing to discuss about it.

It seemed to Arleen that Leland Street was held in a waiting quiet, the kind of quiet that makes one stop and listen; hesitate to walk in the dark; look over one's shoulder for a shadow not of one's own making.

The street slumbered in the hot, sweltering afternoons. A merciless sun beat down; the breeze was negligible, if it came at all. The women haggled with the street peddlers; the old men sat listlessly on the stoops in their undershirts, watching the life of the street move by them.

Miss Horne, the nursing supervisor, sat in her air-conditioned office and looked at Arleen. "It isn't nine o'clock yet and it's ninety in the shade. Don't you envy me sitting here cool, calm and collected?"

Arleen, rechecking her nursing satchel, shook her head. "Nope," she said. "I'd rather be one of the milling herd."

Miss Horne smiled and said wryly, "My words exactly. When you advance to a desk job, you're no longer young; the fire's gone out. I'd rather tackle the heat."

Dr. Rowe sauntered in. "Who'd rather tackle the heat?" he asked.

"We were talking of youth, Doctor," Miss Horne said.

"Ah, youth," Dr. Rowe said. "Precious commodity. People waste it."

"Listen to him philosophize," Miss Horne railed, with gentle irony.

He frowned at her. "If you insist on poking fun at me, I'm going to neglect to ask you out to dinner tonight."

"Dinner?" she said. "Hamburger on a bun? Mustard and catsup on the side?"

"Steak," he said. "Charcoal broiled. A long, cool drink. Air-conditioning."

Miss Horne pretended intense interest. She leaned toward him, hands clasped beneath her chin, lips partly opened. "Tell me more, Doctor!"

Arleen went out into the sweltering street, leaving them still sparring pleasantly with each other. She set her satchel on the car seat behind her, made certain the rear-view mirror was adjusted at the proper angle. The car was serving her well. She hadn't spent a dime on it for repairs since she'd bought it. She thought gratefully of the used-car salesman who had sold it to her.

Both windows were down. She stole a glance at the brash blue sky. Not a sign of rain. She thought how it was after a rain, the fresh, clean smell, as if a giant housekeeper had hosed down the entire earth.

She parked her car in its usual spot. The smell of rotting fruit was a sickening pungency in her nostrils. She saw a gathering of children across the street at the curb, where a fruit peddler had emptied his cart. Arleen recognized some of the Luigui children. Angela was backing away, clutching something against her thin chest. Pietro stood to one side, thumb in mouth, not taking any part in the melee, but watching with greedy, wary eyes.

Arleen let her gaze travel along the street. The sidewalk in front of the poolroom was empty, the Roosters conspicuously absent. As she walked with her usual precise steps toward the tenement that was her destination, she wondered with a quickening of fear if their absence were a bad sign.

She saw that Angela, with curious gentleness, was handing Pietro one of her treasures, a partly rotted orange. But before the little boy could close his fingers around it, it was snatched from his grasp and an older boy was running across the street with it.

Arleen forced herself, with tremendous effort, not to intervene. It did no good; she'd learned that much. The law of the jungle ruled here. Poverty was an ugliness that rotted from the inside out.

The thought of Neelie Ryan was like a freshening breath pressing against her choked lungs.

Neelie was sitting up in bed, looking as excited as a young girl. Her gray hair curled damply across her forehead. She was eager to impart her news.

"Guess what, Miss Anderson? Al worked a day and a half. Of course it wasn't much of a job, maybe, just cleaning out an old storeroom. But they hired him. Oh, it sure did Al good. And you know what? He bought me a present. Look here."

She reached underneath her pillow and brought out a sleazy bedjacket, laced with ribbons, for Arleen's inspection.

She said proudly, "He picked it out all by himself. It was a surprise. He just came in and handed me this package." Tears clouded the bright eyes. "I almost died, I was so happy. I just laid here holding onto the package and bawling!"

She shook her head, and a smile curved her lips upward. "Al kept saying, 'What's the matter, you crazy woman? What are you bawling for?' And I kept saying, 'I'm so happy. Oh, Al, I'm so darn happy I could bawl!' "

Her laughter tinkled out, gay as a child's. "And know what, Miss Anderson? Pretty soon we were both bawling like two crazies!"

There were tears behind Arleen's answering laughter. She thought fiercely, "Why can't she have the chunk of happiness for her and Al? Why can't she?"

Neelie sighed. "Al's a good man," she said. "I'm not saying I don't wish it was different for us. But I wouldn't change Al for no other man in the world, even if I had known it was gonna be like this."

Her worn, thin fingers smoothed the bedjacket as if it were the most precious silk. "That's what love is, Miss Anderson," she told Arleen. "Seeing a person's weaknesses, and loving them anyhow. Feeling their hurts. . . ."

"I know," Arleen said, giving the usual, automatic answer.

Neelie shook her head gently. "No you don't, Miss Anderson," she said. "You ain't knowed real love yet. But one of these days you will, and then you'll understand."

Arleen's firm hands massaged the thin shoulders and neck. "I've been in love," she thought bitterly. "I know what it's like to be hurt." She said lightly, "I've got my job. It's my real love, Neelie."

"No it ain't," the woman argued with gentle insistence. "A man and a woman belong together; that's the way the Lord meant it." Her eyes lit up suddenly.

"That Dr. Wynter," she said, watching Arleen reflectively, "he's a real fine man. Everybody on the street knows what a fine man he is." There was a dreamy look on her face. "My," she said, "that would be nice, wouldn't it? I mean if you two was to like each other that way. A doctor and a nurse—it would be right, wouldn't it?"

Arleen was aware that her laughter trembled around the edges. "Such talk, Neelie!" she chided her. "What are you trying to do, sabotage the nursing profession? Talk me out of my job? There's a shortage of visiting nurses, you know."

"Now, I wasn't meaning nothing like that," Neelie protested. She held out one hand as Arleen gently rubbed the swollen fingers.

"You're real pretty," she said. "And I'll bet Dr. Wynter's seen that. He ain't blind." She chuckled as if she had made a sudden discovery.

"Stop such silly talk," Arleen told her, striving to keep the irritation from showing in her voice, "and give me your other hand."

Neelie's smile was very gentle. "You oughtn't to be ashamed of liking a man, Miss Anderson. You oughtn't to be ashamed at all."

"Oh, Neelie," Arleen chided her, "haven't you anything better to do than lie there and concoct silly love stories?" She began putting her working materials back in her satchel. "Maybe you should have been a writer."

Neelie nodded. She said, "If I'da had the education, I'd have liked something like that fine."

Arleen said, with caustic humor, "Well, you certainly have the imagination for it!"

Irritation rode her as she walked toward her car. It seemed that everyone had but one idea, to throw her and Mark Wynter together! And if she had ever met a man who was totally disinterested in her, it was Dr. Mark Wynter!

Sitting in her car, she got an urgent feeling that she should go to Barney Bonardio's. "Never lie to yourself," she thought, as she headed the car in the direction of Barney's. "The 'urgent feeling' is your desire to see Mark!"

"Of course I won't lie to myself," she said, as if she were carrying on a conversation with someone else. "Naturally I want to see Mark. I want to know about the

Roosters; about Lonnie Michos." She found herself suddenly, fiercely, stubbornly angry.

Why was Mark avoiding her? Didn't she have the right to know what was going on? Hadn't she betrayed Al Ryan's trust and told Mark? The anger was a glowing, bright fire in her when finally she walked into Barney's.

He was listening to a radio at the far end of the counter. When he looked up and saw her, his face creased in a smile. He walked down the counter to her.

"If it ain't the nurse!" he said. "I ain't seen you in a month of Sundays. I was telling my wife that maybe they figured this district was too rough for a little girl like you, and they took you off it."

Arleen grinned. "I'm tougher than I look," she told him. "They've been keeping me busy. I haven't had time for anything except work. Have you anything nice and cold to drink, Barney?"

"How's iced tea strike you?"

Arleen nodded. "Sounds nice and cool."

When he came back with it, in a tall glass, and set it on the counter in front of her, he said, "I suppose you've heard about Dr. Wynter?"

Arleen's heart was colder than the ice in her glass. "What about him?" she asked.

"He got himself all cut up," Barney told her. "He fell into his glass medicine cupboard in the dark. They had to sew him up at the hospital."

Arleen stirred the ice around in her glass. It made clinking sounds against the sides. Her lips were dry and her heart pounded.

"Where is he now?" she asked.

"Oh, they didn't keep him at the hospital." Barney chuckled. "I can see Doc telling them exactly how to sew him up! It must be something, being a doc and having to let another doc go fooling around sewing you up."

Arleen forced herself to drink the iced tea, which she suddenly did not want, because not to do so would hurt Barney's feelings. He was deeply sensitive about the food and drinks he served in the restaurant.

She was aware of a trembling in her legs as she walked out of the restaurant into the blinding white heat of the afternoon.

She could not imagine Mark Wynter's stumbling into his

89

own medicine cupboard, even in the dark. What really had happened?

With fierce determination, she climbed into the car and headed it in the direction of Mark's office.

CHAPTER 15

THERE WAS no one in the waiting room when Arleen walked in. She sat down on the hard bench, got up again, went to the outer door and opened and slammed it hard, then went back and sat down again.

After a few moments the door to the inner office opened and Mark Wynter looked out. He frowned when he saw Arleen. "What are you doing here?"

She got up and went to him. "Barney told me you fell into your medicine cupboard and got cut." Looking at the bandages encasing the lower half of his left arm, she drew a deep, shaky breath. "What really happened, Mark? Did what I told you about the Roosters and Lonnie Michos have something to do with it?"

Mark put his good hand on her shoulder and shook her roughly. "What are you trying to make out of it?" he asked her, his voice tight. "It's exactly as I said it was. I heard someone at the door. I was still half asleep when I got up; I stumbled. That's the way it happened!"

Arleen's shoulder felt curiously empty when Mark took away his hand. She faced him squarely, her eyes searching his.

"Why are you avoiding me?" she asked him, the anger she'd felt earlier trembling in her voice. "Didn't you think I had the right to know what was going on? Don't you think I wondered . . . worried . . . about it?"

Mark's lips tightened with a show of stubbornness. "He's too pale," Arleen thought, a feeling of concern for him rushing through her. "I wonder how much blood he lost? I wonder if he's eating enough?" She chided herself firmly, "That's none of my concern."

"I haven't been avoiding you," Mark began, and then he shook his head. "All right, so perhaps I have been. I don't want you involved. You're a nurse; that's all you're supposed to be. This other is out of your area."

90

"But I *am* involved," Arleen told him. "I've been involved from the moment I first stepped onto Leland Street." She shook her head slowly. "According to your theory, Mark, you shouldn't allow yourself to become involved, either. You're a doctor. Your job is to heal them when they come to you, and no more than that."

Her eyes swept his face; the anger that had touched her earlier was completely gone. "It's a wrong theory," she told him, "that says you can treat their bodies and not become involved in their lives. Some doctors and nurses can achieve that, but not you, Mark, and not me."

Mark Wynter's face softened as if a hand had moved across his face, blotting out the lines and the hardness. His good right hand reached for her and clamped down on her shoulder, gently this time.

The outside door opened and a man lurched in. At his appearance the waiting room suddenly reeked with the sour-sweetness of cheap wine. He staggered to a bench and sank down. His hands hung limply between his spread knees. He didn't raise his head, but his voice moaned his terror. "I'm sick, Doc. Oh, God, but I'm sick!"

Mark's fingers pressed into Arleen's blue-clad shoulder. "Wait," he told her.

She shook her head. "I have to get back to work, Mark."

"I'll see you." His fingers pressed sharply into her shoulder again before he released her. "I'll see you."

Arleen gave an uncertain smile before she turned to leave. It was almost as if he had kissed her!

The heat outside was as blinding hot as ever. But the pounding of her heart had nothing whatever to do with the heat.

As she turned the car to head for the tenement district that lay behind Leland Street, she saw Rose Luigui cross the street at the corner.

Rose seemed to be hurrying, as if she were trying to outdistance someone. She hadn't gone far when Arleen saw three boys step out from between the shelter of some buildings. One of the boys accosted Rose.

Arleen couldn't hear the words, but she could see the angry defiance in Rose's twisted face. And then Rose's hand swept out and slapped the boy a resounding blow across his face. Then she ran as if her life depended on getting away from them.

Arleen's fingers curved around the wheel, trembled. She thought, "What shall I do if they follow her?" The law of

Leland Street said that you did nothing; that you looked the other way.

"I'll get Mark," Arleen decided. "He'll know what to do."

But it wasn't necessary to get Mark. The three watched idly, but made no attempt to go after Rose.

When the boy who had been slapped turned, so that Arleen caught a look at his face, fear spread out from her in ever-widening circles. The thin, cruel face, made more cruel by the fury that twisted it, was that of Lonnie Michos.

There was a sickening dread in Arleen. A slap from a girl was an insult to any boy. To a boy like Lonnie Michos it would become a need to get even. He couldn't afford to let himself be laughed at by the boys with him. He'd have to get back at Rose for the slap!

Arleen almost went back to tell Mark about the episode, then decided against it. Mark had said, "You take everything too much to heart." Perhaps she did. Coming from a small town, she was not yet accustomed to the jungle that was a big-city slum.

Besides, Mark had said, "I'll see you." She'd tell him then, let him decide if the episode meant something or nothing. It wasn't until she was through for the day and getting dinner (it was her week to cook), that she realized Mark had not said when he'd see her. Only that he would.

Had it meant the same as the old, "Don't call me, I'll call you?" Surely Mark wasn't getting the feeling that she was chasing him?

Her cheeks flamed. "Nonsense!" she told herself crisply.

Arleen had difficulty putting what had happened out of her thoughts. She didn't tell Evelyn about the argument between Rose and Lonnie Michos. But she did tell her about Mark's falling into his medicine cupboard and cutting himself.

Evelyn frowned. "Why don't you think it happened the way he said? Why would he lie about it?" She shook her head at Arleen and her lips tightened at the corners.

"The thing is," she said, "you watch too many melodramas on TV. Now you're thinking in terms of melodramas. The old gangster days—'You seen me, boy, and now I'm gonna get you for it. Bang, bang, bang.' And another good guy hits the dust!"

Arleen had to laugh in spite of herself. "You're being terribly silly."

"No kidding?" Evelyn said. "Look who's calling who silly. Boy, would my old English teacher slay me for that one!"

She stretched luxuriously. "I've got a date tonight. That cute intern at the hospital I was telling you about." The carefully arched brows wreathed in a frown. "That'll teach Charley to be working every time I want to go someplace!"

Arleen said, "How can he help it if he has to work?"

Evelyn shrugged. "A man has to learn a woman has some importance."

"Who are you punishing?" Arleen asked her softly. "Charley or yourself?"

Evelyn put both hands on her slender hips and regarded Arleen in amusement. "Now look who's being an analyst! And sweetie, methinks, according to my old English teacher, that it should be 'whom' instead of 'who.' " She shrugged. "Who knows, I might just fall in love with my intern. But then where would I be?"

The night stretched long and unhappy after Evelyn left. Arleen found herself moving restlessly about the small apartment, unable to settle herself to read or even to watch TV.

She was curled up on the sofa, attempting to get interested in a magazine story, when the telephone rang. Thinking it was Charley (Evelyn had told her he might call), she took her time answering it, trying to decide if she should tell him, as Evelyn had advised her to, that she was out with another man, or simply to evade the issue.

She was so intent on its being Evelyn's boy friend that she had difficulty adjusting to the fact of Mark's voice. "Who?" she said. "Who did you say it was?"

Mark sounded impatient and irritated. "Mark Wynter," he said. "Look, are we supposed to be playing some kind of game?"

She apologized contritely. "My roommate's boy friend was supposed to call. I was trying to figure out how to tell him, in a nice way, that's she out on another date."

"Why not tell him the plain truth?" Mark asked. "Why beat around the bush?"

"Because," Arleen said softly, "she's angry at him now, but by tomorrow she'll realize how foolish she's been and want to make up. Why should there have to be hard feelings to be washed away?"

"Well," Mark said, "that's your problem. Are you going to be home tonight? No date?"

"I'm going to be home," Arleen told him. "No date."

"Sure?"

"Sure," Arleen said. The pulse was pounding furiously in her throat. "He sounds like a shy boy," she thought, and a wave of tenderness for him washed through her, frightening her. "I don't want to feel like this about any man," she thought in panic.

"Would you like company?" Mark asked.

Arleen nodded, and then, realizing he couldn't see the nod, she said slowly, "Yes, very much." The way to make sure nothing happens, she assured herself firmly, is to face up to it, not be afraid of it.

"I'll be right over," he said. "I have this hankering to talk to you."

"Look, Mark," Arleen said, "it's quite a distance over here, and you have no car. Couldn't I meet you somewhere?"

Mark said, a tightening in his voice, "Don't you trust me? Are you afraid to be alone with me?"

"Oh, how ridiculous! You've been over here before, haven't you?" She had trouble sweeping the anger from her voice. "I just didn't want you to be inconvenienced."

"Let me worry about that," Mark told her. "You sure you want me to come?"

"I'm sure."

She told herself fiercely, "If he doesn't have the silliest notions!"

"It's safe and secure and peaceful in here," Mark said, sitting on the sofa, nursing a drink. He looked at her sitting across from him in her red-and-black print dress. "You look like a little girl," he added, his voice suddenly rough, "sitting in her living room in some small town, entertaining her boy friend."

The radio had been on when he'd phoned. Arleen hadn't turned it off, only down. A string band was playing soft, dreamy waltz music.

"Shall we dance?" Mark asked.

It wasn't until Arleen started to her feet that she realized he wasn't serious; that his tone was of scornful amusement. With a wave of embarrassment, she settled back again in the chair. Mark had not seemed to notice her movement.

He took a big swallow of his drink, then set it down on the coffee table. He got slowly to his feet, a tall, broad-shouldered, too thin man, with sandy hair that looked in perpetual need of combing.

He moved restlessly about the room, a caged animal in need of freedom. "Up here like this," he said, indicating the room and Arleen, "you can almost fool yourself into thinking the ugliness isn't out there." He gave a vague wave of his hand at the windows that looked out onto the street.

He shook his head bitterly. "No Peter Rossi who could be helped, but won't be. No Lonnie Michos who's going to keep on until he drags himself and the rest of the Roosters into real trouble. No Maggie Brill who's dying of cancer without hope, without future."

He strode over to where Arleen was sitting, and he took hold of her arms and pulled her up so that she stood in front of him. "Why don't you stay up here where it's safe and clean," he flung at her, "and keep your pretty nose out of the rest of it?"

Arleen didn't take offense at his words, or his tone, because she knew the deep hurt inside that had bred them; the helplessness of the man and the doctor to change what was.

What was it Neelie had said? she asked herself silently. "You feel their hurts. . . ." She firmed her lips and pushed the thought away.

"I can't, Mark," she said softly, "any more than you can."

"No," he said. "No, I guess you can't." His eyes boring into hers bruised her, as did his hands straining into the softness of her arms.

She thought for a moment that he was going to kiss her, and her heart shivered in sweet waiting. But then he let her go, walked abruptly over to the window and stared out at the night darkness of the street below.

"What happened to your California beau?" he asked her. "I thought you were going to marry him. I hear he was quite a catch."

Arleen shook her head. "I was never going to marry him, Mark." She remembered what Barney Bonardio had intimated, that Mark was jealous of her!

She searched his face. He gazed back at her coldly. "You're a fool if you turned him down. A girl doesn't always get that kind of security these days. And if you think giving up your own wants and sticking around Leland Street is going to help those people, is going to change any of their lives, then you'd better think again. Because it isn't!"

Arleen felt a coldness in her heart. Barney had been so very wrong in how Mark felt about her. "I'm glad," she told herself. "I don't want him to feel like that about me. I don't want to feel like that about him!"

Then, because she wanted to change the subject, she said, "She slapped him this afternoon. After I left your office."

He stared at her stupidly. "Slapped who? What are you talking about?"

95

"Rose Luigui," Arleen said. "She slapped Lonnie Michos. He said something to her. I couldn't hear what it was, but whatever it was, she slapped him for it."

Mark's scowl deepened. "Rose is Peter's girl," he said, slowly, heavily. "If he insulted her, Peter will have to take care of it with Lonnie. The rest of the gang will be waiting for him to settle with Lonnie."

Arleen stared at him. She'd been wrong. The fury for revenge she'd glimpsed on Lonnie Michos' face had been directed, not at Rose, but at Peter Rossi!

Mark sighed. "I have an idea Lonnie's been wanting a showdown with Peter. I think he arranged this to force Peter into a fight. The small street gangs are much like the bigger organizations. There's always someone aching to take over leadership."

Neither of them had been paying any attention to the radio, but suddenly something the newscaster said caught their attention. "Ten boys who said they were members of a street gang called the Roosters were apprehended in the act of breaking into the office of Dr. Delbert Miller, 12456 Third Avenue. It is believed their purpose was to steal a supply of narcotics which Dr. Miller keeps in his office. The police had been tipped off earlier, and were waiting for them. All of the youths were apprehended."

Mark and Arleen stared at each other. The room was filled with tenseness. "Who tipped off the police?" Mark said. "That's what they're going to be asking when they get out."

Arleen seemed enclosed in a tent of coldness. "Will they think it was Al Ryan? Will they think he told the police, Mark?"

Mark shook his head. "Why would they think that? It would have to be someone on the inside; someone who knew what they planned. Al Ryan wouldn't be that much in the know." He pulled her suddenly to him and said savagely, "Remember you're a nurse. No more than that. Don't try to be!"

Then he let go of her and strode toward the door. Arleen ran after him. "Remember you're a doctor!" she hurled at him. "Don't *you* try to be more than that!"

He looked down at her. And then he raised her chin with savage gentleness, and bent his head. His lips touched hers for only a brief moment, like the whispered end of a song.

After he was gone, Arleen stood where he had left her, her hands clasped in front of her like a child, tears flowing down her cheeks.

CHAPTER 16

THE ATTEMPTED robbery didn't make the headlines. It was a small crime in a city where small crimes and big ones were the accepted daily occurrence. There was to be a closed trial in the judge's chambers, because the boys were all under age.

Mark said he was attending the trial, and Arleen might as well accompany him, since she had insisted on involving herself! The judge permitted them to be there because of their work in the Leland Street area. Miss Gibbons, the social service worker, was also present.

She looked at Arleen and shook her head. "Those are bad boys," she said firmly. "They should be punished. They should be sent someplace where they would learn to respect laws and authority and people. But they won't be. The judge is noted for the softness of his sentences on juveniles. He'll give them a lecture and a second chance. His conscience won't permit him to do anything else. It will be like turning a pack of vicious dogs loose because they haven't yet done anything important enough to merit their destruction!"

Mark disagreed with her. "They need help," he told her, "not punishment. Not in the sense in which you advocate it."

"What other kind is there?" she asked scornfully.

"They need to have help in finding themselves," Mark said carefully. "They need to have their energies directed into the proper channels."

Miss Gibbons said, her voice as careful as Mark's had been, "And will that be accomplished, Dr. Wynter? You know it won't."

The morning sun peeked in through the high windows. The courthouse was old, high domed. The judge's desk was modern, looking almost incongruous in the ancient mustiness of the room.

There was only a sprinkling of parents, and those who were present were sullen and angry, giving the impression that they felt *their* boys were being picked on only because of their poverty.

The boys were restless and uncertain. Without their black

97

leather jackets they looked, to Arleen, naked and helpless, as if the jackets were their strength.

The judge leaned on his desk, frowning at them. "Did you know the doctor kept narcotics in his office? Is that what you were after?"

The boys looked at each other, and at Lonnie Michos. There was a negative shaking of heads.

The judge asked, "Why did you want to rob the doctor's office?"

It was Lonnie who answered. "We thought he'd have something in there we could hock or sell."

"And if you had found narcotics, would you have sold them?" the judge asked, leaning forward to observe them more closely.

Again the negative shaking of heads. Lonnie said, "We wouldn't know who to sell to."

The judge sighed. He directed a glance at one of the arresting officers. "Any signs of addiction?"

The officer shook his head. "No, your honor."

The judge scowled and leaned forward, as if in an attempt to make up his mind. He glanced over the top of his glasses at Miss Gibbons. "You're in social service work in the Leland Street area," he said. "Are you acquainted with the home conditions of any of these boys?"

She nodded. "Six of the families these boys come from are on relief. It's my job to visit the homes." Her voice was grim. "I can only describe the conditions there as deplorable."

There was a muttering among the scattering of parents. "Listen to Miss Big Shot talk!" "Probably her and the judge are in this together!"

The judge pounded with his gavel, and the muttering subsided. Lonnie Michos shuffled his feet, then asked, "Have we got the right to know who informed on us?"

The judge, who had seemed in a reverie, jerked upright. "Who said you'd been informed on?"

"One of my friends' father said he'd read it in the paper," Lonnie came back, not appearing to be at all discomfited.

One of the men seated among the parents nodded. "It was in the paper, all right. I read it."

The judge gave him a frowning glance, and the man lowered his eyes and said no more.

"Why do you want to know who did the informing?" the judge asked Lonnie. "You should be grateful to whomever it was. Because you were apprehended before you could steal anything, the only charge against you is breaking and entering."

His eyes swept from one to the other of the boys in rapid succession. He shook his head. "None of you boys has a court record. I'm going to give you another chance." His voice hardened. "But if any of you come before me on any charge again, I'm going to sentence you. And it won't be the minimum sentence I can give you, but the maximum!"

Arleen said, when they were outside on the street again, "Peter wasn't with them."

Mark shrugged. "He wouldn't be in on something like that. The kids were after narcotics. The judge knew it, too, but there was no proof. Maybe he thinks the scare of being sentenced next time will keep them out of that kind of trouble." He shook his head. "But it won't faze them, I'm afraid. A kid like Lonnie isn't going to mind having a court record. It would only set him up bigger in his own eyes."

Arleen said, a coldness washing over her, "He wanted to know who had informed on them. He'll find out, Mark. He'll make it his business to find out. And then . . . and then. . . ." Her voice shook in her throat. "Do you think Al Ryan. . . ."

"No," Mark said. "Al's not the kind to go running to the police. If he knew anything, he'd keep his mouth shut, the same as the others in that neighborhood. No, whoever it was, it wasn't Al Ryan."

They walked to Arleen's car. "I'll drive you to your office," Arleen offered.

Mark shook his head. "It's out of your way. Besides, it's a nice day, and I want to walk. I think better when I'm walking."

Suddenly he stared. Arleen, following his stare, saw Rose Luigui and Peter Rossi on the opposite side of the street. They seemed to be arguing.

Rose was wearing the tight skirt and blouse she always affected. Her black hair was piled atop her head in what Arleen could only describe in her own mind as a ridiculously exaggerated hairdo. Spike heels completed her costume.

Peter Rossi wore the inevitable T-shirt and tight jeans. He had left off the black leather jacket with its insignia. Whether it was in respect for the ten who could not wear it in court, Arleen didn't know.

She said, "Peter and Rose must have come to the trial and couldn't get in. Why would they want to come, Mark?"

Mark shrugged. "Various reasons. The best guess I can

99

hazard is that Peter, being the leader of the Roosters, might have decided it would be good politics to be there. On the other hand, it could be that the gang figures what one is in on, the others are in on, too."

He waited until she was in the car. "Forget about it," he advised her. "If Peter thinks Lonnie should be taken care of, he'll do it. He wouldn't welcome any help from you. And neither would Rose Luigui."

As they said good-by and Arleen headed the car in the direction of her next stop, she knew that Mark was right, and that her help would not be welcomed, no matter how sincerely she offered it.

When she arrived at the apartment that night, she was pleasantly surprised to find a letter from Guy Newman.

He wrote that he had succeeded in his venture; that everything was "in the bag." He would be in Detroit in perhaps three or four days, with a stop-off in Saltboro, of course!

"Keep your heart open for me," he wrote, "and don't let anyone slip in while I'm gone. I haven't changed. I still judge every other girl by you, and they all lose in the judging."

When Arleen finished the letter, she burst into tears.

Evelyn said, alarmed, "Bad news?"

Arleen said, "He's in love with me!"

Evelyn stared at her stupidly. "Who?"

"Guy Newman!"

"Well, for pete's sake," Evelyn said, "that's something to cry about? Now I've heard just about everything."

Arleen wiped her eyes. She knew she'd acted more than a little foolish. "It's just that I'm so tired," she explained. "Everything's been happening today." Her mouth shook. "I don't want him to be in love with me!" she protested.

Evelyn hooted gently, "Listen, sweetie, you might as well expect the sun not to set, as to expect to keep a man from falling in love with the one he's picked out to fall in love with. So don't worry about it."

"I'm sorry I acted so silly," Arleen said, lamely.

Evelyn shrugged. "You get touched too easily, sweetie." She held out her left hand, fluttering her fingers, trying for Arleen's attention.

Arleen noticed the ring. "Charley?"

Evelyn nodded happily. She said, "I told you a woman had to make a man know she's important."

It was nearly three o'clock the next afternoon before Ar-

100

leen looked in on Neelie Ryan. She found the woman not nearly so cheerful and gay as usual. And she was flushed. Arleen had a moment of wondering what would happen to Al Ryan if Neelie were forced to spend time in a hospital.

But Neelie's temperature proved to be normal. "Are you having much pain, Neelie?" Arleen asked gently.

Neelie shook her head. "The pills Dr. Wynter gives me take care of that pretty good, and with you coming and rubbing me all the time, the pain don't hardly amount to nothing."

Arleen probed gently. "Neelie, if it isn't the pain that's bothering you, what is it? You aren't your usual self."

The woman's mouth twisted. "I know, Miss Anderson," she said. "It's Al. He went out and he ain't come back. I can't think what coulda happened to him."

"How long has he been gone?" Arleen asked.

"Almost two hours now," Neelie said, anxiety evident in her voice. "Al never stays away like that. He goes out for a few minutes, sometimes as much as a half hour, but no more. He worries when he's gone for fear I'll need him."

Arleen said, "He could have had the chance to do an odd job, and he took it."

Neelie shook her head. "I know what you're thinking. You're thinking that Al does all that drinking, and if he got too much he wouldn't worry about how long he'd been gone. But Al don't do no drinking outside. He brings his bottle home and sits in the chair and drinks it until it's gone. He wouldn't go out and get drunk and leave me here. Al's not like that."

Arleen said, "If something had happened to him, Neelie, you'd know. The police would let you know."

"Sure," Neelie said, uncertainly, "I guess they would, at that. I guess maybe it's like you said, and Al got a chance to do a bit of work, and he took it, and there wasn't no way he could let me know."

She gave a pale imitation of her usually infectious laugh. "Maybe he'll bring me home a nightgown to match that bedjacket he brought me. And I told him not to spend no more money on me. I told him I got everything I need."

Arleen was filled with such pity that it threatened to break through her chest. No matter how much faith Neelie had in Al, a man who drank as Al Ryan drank could not be depended upon. If someone were to offer him a few drinks in a bar, he would stay as long as the buying continued. Arleen was sure of that—and wished she weren't.

She worried over Neelie. She hesitated about leaving her alone, but she had other patients to see in the course of the afternoon. She said, "I hate having to leave you here by yourself, Neelie."

Neelie made a great show of cheerfulness. "Oh, you don't need to worry none about me, Miss Anderson. Al'll be here pretty soon."

Arleen said, "I'll send someone up to stay with you until he comes."

"No need to do that, Miss Anderson."

Arleen touched the small, swollen hand, and said, affection in her voice, "Don't worry about your husband, Neelie. He'll be back."

Neelie nodded. "Sure," she said, "I know he will."

Arleen thought, "I pretended to Neelie that I was so sure about finding someone to stay with her. But who am I going to find?"

As luck would have it, she saw Angela in the hall outside the Luigui apartment. She beckoned to her, and the child came over shyly.

"Angela," Arleen said, "you're a big enough girl to go upstairs and sit with Mrs. Ryan until her husband comes home, aren't you?" She pressed a quarter into the small grimy palm.

Angela looked at the money and nodded, wide-eyed. "You won't leave until Mr. Ryan comes home, will you?" Arleen asked.

Angela shook her head. Arleen thought, "I'm like Mark; I have to pay first and hope she'll do the job asked of her."

As she walked toward her car, she was filled with fury toward Al Ryan. But she was not concerned about him. She was only angry because he was causing Neelie needless worry.

CHAPTER 17

IT WAS Evelyn who told her about Al Ryan. She came home from the hospital only minutes after Arleen walked in the door of the apartment. She didn't sail her hat and purse at the sofa as she usually did. She seemed in a sober, reflective mood, so much so that Arleen gave her a sharp glance.

"Something went wrong at the hospital?"

Evelyn shook her head. "I don't want to upset you," she said, "and it may not be the same one at all. But I was on emergency service today, and an Al Ryan was brought in about two hours ago. He'd had a severe beating—although he denied that's what it was. He said he'd fallen down a flight of stairs and knocked himself out."

Arleen's heart pounded. She felt herself go pale. "Al Ryan?" she stammered. "Neelie's Al?"

"I don't know," Evelyn said. "I've heard you talk so much of the Ryans, and when this man came in, with the same name and all, I couldn't help but wonder."

Arleen drew her eyes away from Evelyn's face and walked quickly to the telephone. She was making a mountain out of a molehill. There must be more than one Al Ryan in a city the size of Saltboro!

She dialed Mark Wynter's number, her finger shaking against the circles on the dial.

She thought he wasn't going to answer, and then his voice came on, crisp and impersonal sounding. Arleen's hand was white around the knuckles from the pressure with which she gripped the phone.

"Mark?" she said. "This is Arleen Anderson. My roommate just told me that an Al Ryan. . . ."

"Was brought into the hospital a few hours ago," Mark said.

Arleen's grip on the phone tightened. She said, unhappily, "Then it was Neelie's Al. I hoped. . . ."

Mark said, "Have you eaten yet? If you haven't, I'll take you out and buy you a hamburger. Of course, if you've something better than that on the menu at home. . . ."

"I'm not hungry," Arleen said. "Mark, does Neelie know?"

"She had to know."

"Is there anyone with her?" Arleen asked.

"Rose Luigui."

"Rose?" Arleen couldn't keep the astonishment out of her voice.

"There was no one else I could find."

Arleen thought she detected a puzzled note in his voice. "She didn't put up any argument when I asked her to stay with Neelie. Instead, it was almost as if . . . she felt responsible." Arleen could almost see him shaking his head.

"You never did tell me whether or not you've eaten," he chided her.

"I haven't eaten," Arleen said, "but I'm not hungry."

"I'll be there as soon as I can make it," he told her. "I'm not hungry, either, but you can't call a hamburger really eating."

Evelyn was sympathetic when Arleen turned from the phone. "Then it was the same Al Ryan?"

Arleen nodded. She felt choked. "Poor Neelie," she said. "What's she going to do now?"

"He isn't going to die," Evelyn told her. "He's pretty badly banged up, but it's not that serious. He's only being kept overnight in the hospital for observation, but the admitting doctor said he's running the chance of a liver infection."

She shook her head at Arleen. "Don't look like that. He didn't mean from the beating, he meant from the stuff Al drinks."

Arleen sighed. "He's really a good man, it's just that he gets discouraged. He's old and there are no jobs for him, and Neelie's sick and he can't do anything for her. . . ."

Evelyn put both hands on her shoulders, and shook her gently. "They aren't your life, so stop trying to make them your life. You've got enough to do taking care of yourself." She scowled at Arleen. "I told you in the beginning that Dr. Wynter would be bad for you!"

Mark had to insist Arleen have a hamburger and coffee. He said fiercely, "Do you think going without food is going to help either Al or Neelie? You're a grown-up, mature woman, or at least you're supposed to be! Stop acting like a child."

His voice was rough and it stirred anger in Arleen. She glared at him.

A ghost of a grin touched one corner of his lips. "At least I've aroused you out of your lethargy."

He wouldn't let her talk until she had finished half of her hamburger. And then he leaned toward her across the booth. "What do you think about Al?"

Arleen's hand, touching the handle of her cup, shook. She said fiercely, "I'm sorry for him, but it was a terrible thing for him to do to Neelie, going out and getting drunk like that and putting himself in a position where someone could beat him up!"

Mark shook his head at her. "What kind of story are

104

you trying to sell yourself?" he asked her. "Al Ryan wasn't drunk when he was brought into the hospital. I talked to the admitting doctor."

Arleen's lips shook. She had to bring to the front of her mind what she had desperately tried to deny—that the Roosters were responsible for Al Ryan's beating!

She said slowly, staring, as if fascinated, into Mark's serious face, "For some reason they thought it was Al who informed on them. It is that, isn't it, Mark?"

He didn't answer her. "They found Al in an alley off Third Avenue," he said, "behind a bar, only two blocks from where the doctor's office was broken into. Al sometimes swept up and did odd jobs for the bartender. He'd give him a bottle of cheap wine for his work." He frowned in concentration.

"Lonnie Michos could have seen Al near the bar; he could have decided that Al had found out about his plans, and gone to the police with his information."

His voice was bitter. "It wouldn't matter to Lonnie whether or not he believed this about Al. He needed a goat. He had to have someone to blame for the leak to the police. The Roosters needed to have someone to blame for it."

Arleen stared at him, her lips dry and her heart pounding. She said, "Will the judge sentence Lonnie now, Mark? Will he be sent someplace where he can't influence other boys? Where perhaps he can be helped himself?"

Mark shook his head. He said, despair in his voice, "Al swears he fell down a flight of stairs. I talked to him, and he won't change his story. There is no proof against Lonnie Michos or any of the other Roosters."

Arleen didn't have to ask Mark why Al Ryan refused to talk. She had been around Leland Street long enough to know that the way to live in peace was to say nothing, see nothing, do nothing.

She stared with distaste at the rest of the hamburger. "Mark, I can't possibly eat any more."

"All right," Mark said. He leaned across the booth top and touched the tip of her nose with the end of one finger. "The world is still revolving," he said. "It's not the end of everything." He slid toward the end of the booth. "Let's go see Neelie."

Arleen nodded. Mark drove her car. He drove carefully and swiftly through the heavy nighttime traffic. "Al's shook up," he told her, "but he has no broken bones. Neelie has the strength to pull him out of this. You don't have to worry about her."

As the noise and clutter of the city seemed to literally engulf the car, Arleen felt a sudden need for her mother, and for the clean, fresh normalcy of her former life.

"We used to have strawberry shortcake every night," she said, "from early June until the end of the strawberry season. My mother used to ask what my father and I wanted for dessert each night, and she'd sigh and throw up her hands and say, 'Don't tell me, let me guess! Strawberry shortcake?' "

Arleen's laughter quivered. Mark reached over and squeezed her hand nearest him, as if he had understood her need to remember the good things, in order to dispel the crushing weight of the big city, where slums flourished and violence was a way of life.

They found Neelie sitting up in bed, her hands clasped on the thin blanket that covered her. The bulb, dangling from the ceiling, was encased in a clip-on shade, and it sent a pale, yellowish light downward. At their entrance, Rose Luigui looked up. Her lips wore their usual sullen downward cast, but there was a glimmer of fear in the dark eyes that swept Arleen's face with a show of indifference.

Arleen went to Neelie and bent over her. "Al's all right," she told her gently. "He'll be coming home tomorrow. They did tell you, didn't they?"

Neelie nodded, her eyes too bright. Her lips quivered just a bit at the edges. "I prayed," she said. "I prayed as hard as I knew how when Al didn't come home. When the policeman came, I knew it was about Al, but I knew he wasn't dead. I knew the Lord wouldn't do that to me and Al."

She looked so small, so infinitely tired, so pathetic in her intensity, that Arleen had difficulty in holding back the tears.

Neelie pleated a fold of the blanket between a thumb and forefinger. "The policeman who came said he thought Al had been mugged, being found in an alley and all."

Mark said quietly, "Al told me he fell down a flight of stairs."

"Oh?" Neelie said carefully. "Well, Al ought to know, I guess."

"Neelie," Arleen said fiercely, "both Dr. Wynter and I think Al is lying. We think he. . . ."

Rose Luigui's voice broke in shrilly. "Let her alone! Like

106

she said, he ought to know what happened to him, oughtn't
he?" Her voice shook with the intensity of her anger. "Listen, nurse lady, why don't you let us alone here? Nobody
asked you to butt into things. Why don't you just do your
nursing and keep your nose out of the rest of it?"

Neelie said, "That's no way to talk to Miss Anderson!"
She shot a glance at Arleen. "But she's right, you know. I
guess Al ought to know what happened to him. I'm satisfied, and he is too. Don't bother about it." There was pleading in her voice. "Please."

Mark had not closed the door behind him when he and
Arleen had entered the room. "Well, if it's not a family
gathering," Peter Rossi's voice said from the open doorway.

He stood with his usual slouch, his dark eyes surveying
the room coolly. But Arleen noticed something different
about him, a wary tenseness the boy had not had before.

Rose jumped to her feet. "Well," she said, "I've got to
go. Me and Peter got a date."

Mark frowned. He said, "I thought you'd spend the night
with Mrs. Ryan; that you'd stay with her until her husband comes home tomorrow."

Rose shrugged. "Maybe I might have done it, except I've
got this date with Peter, and I don't intend to break it.
Not for anyone!" She glared defiance at Mark.

Peter Rossi stepped into the room, walking with a natural,
animal grace. "You stay with her," he told Rose. "She ain't
in no position to be left here all by herself."

Rose shrilled at him, "Listen to the big boss man! Thinking he can tell me what I can or can't do!"

Neelie said, her voice distressed, "It's all right. I don't
need no one."

Peter stepped to the side of Neelie's bed and looked
down at her. "Rose is just talking," he said. "She's going
to stay. She wants to stay." He looked up, glaring at the
girl. "Ain't that right?"

Rose's full, red lips tightened, but she nodded sullenly.

"Well," Peter said, "that's more like it." He walked,
swaggering a little, toward the door. "Be seeing all of you
nice folks."

Rose got ahead of him and stood in the doorway, barring
his way. "Where do you think you're going?"

Peter's thin, handsome face reddened. "This ain't your
old lady you're talking to!" he told her, grimly. "I don't
have to tell any doll my business or where I'm going or
when I'll be back!"

Arleen saw Rose's lips quiver. "I suppose you're going to do some crazy thing now!" she flung at him. "You haven't got any more sense than to do that!" She put her hands on her hips and glared at him. "I suppose you think that'll make you somebody, huh? Well, it will, all right! You'll get yourself killed, that's what happens to big-shot brave guys!"

Peter pushed her, not too gently, out of his way and walked out of the room.

Arleen and Mark looked at each other. It was Arleen who said gently to Rose, "Why are you afraid for Peter? What is he planning on doing?"

The girl shook her head. "Get out of here and let me alone!" But there was no fire in her anger.

Arleen hesitated. It was Neelie who said gently, "Do what she says, Miss Anderson. Please."

Walking down the steep, dark stairs, Arleen said to Mark, "What is it, Mark? What's going on? Whatever it is, Rose is desperately afraid for Peter."

Mark drew her out onto the sidewalk when they reached the downstairs hall. He said carefully, "I don't know." His hand brushed at her cheek. "This is no storybook land, Arleen, and we aren't storybook characters who solve mysteries and make dreams come true for the other characters in our book, or punish the bad and bring fortune to the good."

He took hold of her by one arm and led her toward her car. "There's no way we can make them let us in, when they don't want us let in," he told her. "The very worse thing anyone can do with these kids is to try to force his way into their confidence. That has to be given."

He got in behind the wheel of the car. "I'm going to drive you home, park your car for the night, take you up to your apartment, kiss you good night, and hope you get a good night's sleep. And then I'm going home and hope the same for myself."

CHAPTER 18

ARLEEN FELT the tenseness the moment she parked her car in her usual place on Leland Street. Outwardly it looked the same. Children fought and scrambled over the rotting fruit and vegetables last night's peddlers had dumped into the gutter. Old men shuffled along the street listlessly, on their morning outing; a few pale-faced boys, no more than nine or ten, searched avidly for thrown-away cigarette butts.

A coldness that was like a warning moved in slow waves up Arleen's back. She had no reason for such feelings; no ghostly figures had jumped at her out of the early-morning brightness. She tried to joke herself out of her anxiety, but could not.

It was one of the more pleasant days during June. The sky, above the crumbling buildings and shabby rooftops, was a country sky, warm and blue and generously encompassing.

Arleen had not slept well. There were violet smudges beneath her blue eyes, and a tired droop to her mouth. Dr. Rowe had teased her this morning that she should marry the guy, so she could go home and get the necessary sleep. "A husband never keeps you up too late," he told her. "Only a beau does that."

Angela Luigui, trying to find a good spot in the rotted banana she had snatched from the heap in the gutter, saw Arleen and gave her shy smile.

"Rose is crying." She offered the information cheerfully.

Arleen frowned. "Is there some reason she's crying, Angela?"

The little girl nodded. "Peter hit her," she said.

"Peter Rossi?" Arleen was puzzled and disbelieving.

"I guess so," Angela said, and then, as if bored with the subject, she went racing down the sidewalk.

There was discouragement in Arleen. She hadn't taken Peter Rossi for the kind of boy who would hit a girl. She sighed as she walked. Mark had certainly been right. This was not storybook land, and you could not write the happy endings.

She saw Rose Luigui at the top of the second-floor landing. The girl was wiping her eyes with the back of one hand. She glanced up at Arleen, and then deliberately turned her face away and made a wide circle to avoid her.

Arleen hesitated. Then what Mark had said pushed its way into her mind. "The very worse thing you can do with these kids is to try and push your way into their confidence."

She kept on her way along the hall to the third-floor stairs. "Even when Rose was not in trouble," Arleen thought, "she avoided and scorned me. So why should I think she would wish to tell me anything now?"

The discouragement deepened into despair. What had she

accomplished with these people? "The Angel of Leland Street." Was that a title she craved? She jeered at herself in fierce, bitter scorn. Rose Luigui was right. She should do her nursing and let anything else alone!

She hesitated outside the Luigui door. She hadn't been to see Anna or baby Carmella in days. With sudden resolution, she knocked on the door.

Anna, opening the door, stared at her vacantly. It took no expert to know she'd been drinking.

Arleen sighed. It was not the time to ask Anna about her six weeks' check-up. She smiled coolly at the woman. "I've come to see the baby," she told her calmly, "and to check up on Pietro."

Anna swayed drunkenly, "So check up, okay. So check up."

Arleen found Carmella fed, relatively clean and dry. Rose's work, she thought; surely not that of Anna.

Pietro too, had a fairly clean face. His cleanliness ended at his chin, but Arleen could see that the disfiguring blotches and scaly patches on his face were rapidly clearing up.

Arleen wondered about Rose. She knew enough about Anna to know that Pietro's relative cleanliness was also of Rose's doing. She remembered what Mark had said of Rose, that she, like Peter Rossi had the qualities to become more than she was, but would not, because the chance she needed would not come for her.

Arleen thought fiercely, "It's not my doing, and there's nothing I can do to change it. So why don't I accept it?"

Anna followed her to the door. She opened it and stood lurching against it. Rose Luigui was still in the hall. She was leaning up against the wall near the stairs. She had the appearance of someone waiting for someone . . . or something to happen.

Anna made a belching sound low in her throat. "See her?" she pointed a shaky finger in Rose's direction. "There's my big-shot daughter, too good for her mama. Know what kind of friends she's got, huh? Stoolies. That's what she's got for a boy friend! A stoolie!"

Rose screamed at her, "Shut up, you! Shut your filthy mouth! Shut up!"

Anna laughed in drunken pleasure. "Listen to her, taking up for him. Turns his own gang in. Know what? Turns them in! What kind of boy's that, you answer me, nurse.

What kind of boy does something like that? Goes running to the cops!"

Arleen walked away from her. She began now to understand the tenseness that had made itself felt the moment she'd stepped out onto Leland Street.

She touched Rose's arm, and said with fierce determination, "What is she talking about?"

Rose merely glowered at her, but the fright was visible behind the bravado.

Arleen said sternly, "Is she talking about Peter Rossi? Did he inform on the Roosters? Is that what you were afraid of last night, that he'd be found out?" Scorn sounded in her voice. "He did that, and he let that old man take the blame and the beating for him! What kind of boy is he?"

Rose's pretty face tightened. She said, "Listen, nurse lady, you don't know what you're talking about, any more than my old lady does! Sure, Peter informed. He didn't want the Roosters starting on heroin. When he found out what they were up to he went to the cops. But it was to protect them!"

Her lips quivered, and for a second she was only a very frightened and helpless young girl. "At the trial he wanted to tell what he'd done. He wanted them to know he was the one!" Her voice shook. "He's crazy! I had to make him listen to me and not do such a crazy thing! He didn't know they'd think it was Mr. Ryan."

She drew a deep breath, and the hardness returned to her face. "He told them last night. He wouldn't listen to me. He's crazy. He won't listen to nobody. I told him they wouldn't touch Mr. Ryan any more. I told him it was over and done with, and there was no sense in him acting the big-shot hero when it was already done and over! But he wouldn't listen. He went and told them, the whole gang! He told them he'd squealed on them!"

She shook her head. "They'll get him," she said, an utter hopelessness in her voice. "They're all with Lonnie now. Even the ones who don't belong to the Roosters are against Peter. It doesn't matter why he did what he did. He's still a squealer. He went to the cops! He hasn't got a friend left on the street!" Her voice quavered. "Except me. I know what made him do it. The others don't care! They're all like Ma . . . yelling 'squealer' at him!"

Arleen thought, "I've never seen Rose like this before. I didn't know she could be like this." Mark had known, she thought.

111

Arleen knew that she could go only so far, and if she pushed for Rose's friendship, it would be withdrawn at once. She said softly, "You forget Dr. Wynter and me."

When Rose didn't answer her, Arleen did not press the point, but went on upstairs to Neelie Ryan's apartment. She could hear Anna still railing drunkenly at Rose.

When she walked into the Ryan apartment, a surprise greeted her. She knew Al was home, so she was prepared to see him sitting propped up on a chair, the bandages still on both arms and on the left side of his face.

But she was unprepared for Neelie, pushing herself, with the aid of a straight-backed chair, from her bed to where Al sat.

Arleen was aware that the shock she felt showed through in her voice. "Neelie," she said, "what in the world are you doing up on your feet?"

The woman's eyes shone with a certainty and happiness they had lacked the night before. "Al's home, Miss Anderson. Ain't that grand? He's home, and I'm making him sit and me do for him for a change."

Arleen frowned, and Al Ryan said quickly, in an emotion-charged voice, "You make her get some sense. I've yelled myself hoarse at her and she won't listen. The only way I can make her get back in that bed where she belongs is by picking her up and throwing her in it, and I ain't got that kind of strength yet."

Neelie laughed, as if she were thoroughly happy. "Listen to him talk," she said. "Listen, Al, didn't I tell you that if ever the time came when you needed me, I could get up out of that bed and take care of you? Well, I proved it, didn't I?"

Al shook his head. "Neelie, Neelie!" He appealed to Arleen. "She's gonna hurt herself, hobbling around like that. You tell her!"

Arleen pursed her lips. "No, she won't hurt herself," she said. "In fact, it's good for her to exercise her legs, if she can manage it." She looked at Neelie. "Does Dr. Wynter know what you're up to?"

Neelie shook her head. "He ain't been around today."

Arleen said firmly, "Well, he will be. I'll see that he knows what's going on here."

She set down her satchel and took hold of Neelie with her firm, young arms. "All right," she said, "back to bed you go. It's been months since you've been out of that bed. I don't see how you managed it."

112

Neelie said with utmost surety, "Why, I figured Al needed me, and I just plain told the good Lord He'd have to let me get up on my feet."

Arleen shook her head. "Neelie!" Her throat was choked with pity and affection.

Neelie said, "Al won't eat nothing. I was going to fix him some soup when you came along."

"I'll fix it for him," Arleen said.

As she heated the soup, she threw in, with apparent casualness, "It was quite a thing Peter Rossi did, wasn't it?"

Neelie asked gently, "What was it he did, Miss Anderson?"

"Oh," Arleen said, "he went to the police when he found out that some of the Roosters were planning to steal heroin from a doctor's office. He had the police waiting for them."

"Oh?" Neelie said. And then softly, "Well, I guess he did the right thing, all right. But I don't know how the Roosters are going to take it, once they find out."

"They know Peter did it," Arleen said, carefully. "He told them last night."

Arleen heard a choked sound from Al Ryan, but she didn't turn around.

Neelie shook her head. She said, distressed, "Oh, my, he shouldn't have done that!"

Arleen turned slowly to face Al Ryan. "Mr. Ryan," she said, "now you can tell the truth about what really happened to you. It was Lonnie Michos and some of the Roosters, wasn't it? They waylaid you and beat you up, because they had an idea you had found out their plans and gone to the police. Isn't that the truth of it?"

Arleen saw the look Al and Neelie exchanged. "I told the truth," Al said, coldly. "I fell down a flight of stairs and banged myself up."

Neelie nodded. "Al told me how it was, Miss Anderson." There was that note of pleading in her voice again. "I guess Al knows how it happened to him, don't you think, Miss Anderson?"

Arleen sighed and poured Al's soup into a bowl. They weren't going to change their story, no matter what. They both felt safe with it, and they were going to stick with it.

She wanted to ask Mark about Neelie, so she went straight to his office when she left the tenement. She found no one in the waiting room, and when she decided to look inside the inner office, she found that also empty.

She decided there was only one sure place to find Mark,

and that was at Barney Bonardio's. But when she arrived at Barney's, Mark was not there, and had not been there.

Barney, usually happy to see her, frowned at her appearance. "You shouldn't be wandering around by yourself, Miss Anderson."

Arleen said pleasantly, "I'm not exactly wandering around, Barney. Dr. Wynter isn't in his office. I thought he might be here."

Barney shook his head. "I ain't seen him today."

Arleen ordered coffee. "I'll wait a few moments," she said. "He might come in."

She sipped at her coffee. There was no one else in the restaurant. She tried to bring the conversation around to Peter Rossi and the Roosters, but Barney deftly sidetracked her.

"Know what me and my wife was talking about this morning? Trying to sell this place and buying us a piece of land out in the sticks and building ourselves some kind of house on it." His eyes wandered toward the door. "Hey, you didn't wait in vain. Here's the doc now."

Arleen swiveled around on her stool and watched Mark walk toward her. He swung up on a stool beside her. "Coffee," he said.

He swung his gaze to Arleen. Before he could say anything, she asked, "I suppose you know about Peter Rossi?"

When he nodded, she said fiercely, "What's going to happen to him now?"

"I don't know," Mark admitted.

"Why did he do it?"

Mark shrugged. "Maybe because he was afraid for Al and Neelie; maybe because he wanted them to know it was him."

Arleen said, her voice low and tight, "Rose is afraid for Peter. She tried to keep him from telling. She says the Roosters will get Peter for informing; that nobody on the street is his friend now." Her eyes widened. "They'll be after Rose, too, won't they, Mark? She's Peter's girl."

"I have some friends on the force," Mark said. "I've asked them to keep a careful eye on the Roosters' doings, and to keep Peter and Rose in sight as much as possible." He tried to smile at her. "Nothing's going to happen, not with the police watching out for them."

But Arleen knew he didn't believe that any more than she did. It wasn't until later that she realized she had forgotten to tell him about Neelie.

A telegram from Guy Newman was waiting for her, back at the apartment. It said that Guy would pick her up at nine for dinner. Arleen almost cried. She certainly didn't feel up to coping with Guy tonight.

CHAPTER 19

GUY NEWMAN looked bronzed and confident. He leaned toward Arleen, taking both of her hands in his. "I've missed you," he said softly.

Evelyn, dressed for her date, stopped on her way out the door. "If I didn't have this thing for Charley," she told Guy, "I could go for you myself. You're the cutest!"

Guy grinned at her. "Don't think I haven't been noticing what a cute chick you are, too."

Evelyn grinned. "Now, there," she said airily to Arleen, "is a most observing man." She waved a hand at them. "Have a nice time, you two," and went out the door, closing it loudly behind her.

Arleen said wryly, "Evelyn always slams things."

Guy said, "Let's talk about you and me. You look like an angel in that white dress."

A heavy hand hit against Arleen's heart. "Angel of Leland Street." She tried to close the door on that part of her mind. She didn't want to think about any of it! On a date you were supposed to have fun. She owed that much to Guy, didn't she?

"I'm not an angel," she told him lightly.

His eyebrows raised ever so slightly. "I'm glad," he said. "I wouldn't know how to handle an angel. Now, as to where you would like to go. . . ."

"Someplace nice and quiet, with soft music," Arleen said.

His eyes searched her face. "You feel like that?"

Arleen thought unhappily, "I've given him the wrong impression."

Guy sat in a padded booth across from her at the Safari. "How do you like it?"

Arleen nodded. "Nice." A string orchestra played in the background; pink lights shed a soft glow.

115

"Besides the proper atmosphere," Guy told her, "I've heard they serve the most delicious and exotic food."

He ordered baby lobster. "Have you ever eaten it?" he asked Arleen. "It's really good." He offered her a piece, which she declined.

"I'm afraid I'm not the exotic food type," she told him, suppressing a shudder. She had ordered chicken.

She tried desperately to act as if she were enjoying herself, but she failed utterly. At the end of the meal, Guy laid aside his knife and fork and leaned toward her across the table. "What's wrong, Arleen?" he asked quietly. "You're pretending a pleasure you aren't feeling. When you suggested a quiet spot for dinner, I had the hope it was because of romantic feelings toward me. That isn't true, is it?"

"No," Arleen admitted miserably.

The waiter removed their plates and brought fresh coffee. Guy took her hands in his. "Is it about another man, Arleen?"

"No," she protested. "It isn't anything like that, Guy." Her under lip quivered, and for one horrible moment she was afraid her overwrought nerves would give way and she would burst into tears.

Some couples were getting up to dance. "Let's dance," Arleen said.

Guy nodded, respecting her wish not to talk about what was bothering her.

When they returned to their booth, the coffee was cold. "I'd rather dance than drink coffee," Arleen said, with a terrible attempt at gaiety.

The waiter quietly removed the coffee cups and brought fresh, hot coffee. Guy lit a cigarette. "You're one of the few girls I know who don't smoke," he told Arleen.

She shrugged. "I never picked up the habit," she said. She closed her eyes for a moment to listen to the music without other distractions. "They play nicely," she said.

Guy nodded. "I have to go back to California in a few days," he said, staring at the glowing tip of his cigarette. "We're enlarging the plant. We need more trained young men to work in the factory. We're going to set up a training unit and I've got to be there to supervise things."

Arleen stared at him, gripped suddenly with a highly improbable idea. Her eyes sparkled as she leanded across the booth top, intent on selling Guy the idea.

"These young men you're going to train," she said, "is there any special requirement? Do they have to be high-school graduates or anything like that?"

Guy's eyes narrowed on her face. "Not particularly," he said, "but I'd prefer that they were." He frowned. "You're working up to something, Arleen. What is it?"

Arleen shook her head, the sparkle gone out of her eyes. "It was a crazy thought," she said. "I don't want to involve you in it. Let's forget it."

"That's woman reasoning. You've already involved me by arousing my curiosity. So, out with it."

Arleen told him, in an emotion-heavy voice, of Peter Rossi and what he had done; of the Roosters and their need to get revenge on him; of Rose Luigui who loved and was afraid for Peter.

She sighed. "Peter's very intelligent, Guy, and he's sensitive. He wanted desperately to go to high school, but his step-father stopped that for him. He used to beat Peter and Peter's mother. It's left deep wounds on Peter, but I'm sure that all he needs is a chance—" her eyes held Guy's—"and someone who believes in him, and understands what it's like to fight your way out of the slums."

Guy stubbed out his cigarette. "You're building up a strong case for him, aren't you, Arleen? Are you trying to work on my pity, because I was a slum boy myself? It won't work, you know. This Peter has to have something on the ball before I'd lift a hand to help him."

Arleen said, with deep earnestness, "Will you see him, Guy? Will you talk to him? Someone helped you climb out of the pit. Wouldn't it be right for you to help someone else to make the climb?"

"All right," he said, "I'll see him. I won't make you any promises, Arleen, but I'll talk to him."

She smiled happily, "Thank you, Guy. I can have him at the Ryan apartment at two tomorrow. I have to go there to take care of Neelie. Would two o'clock be all right for you?"

Guy nodded. "Neelie Ryan—that wouldn't be the woman who has this great dream of seeing the swallows come to Capistrano, would it? The woman whose husband wants to grow flowers all year long?" He shook his head and added slowly, "You wouldn't be thinking that I could also use a gardener for my factory, would you, Arleen? I suppose a thought like that never occurred to you?"

Arleen's eyes widened. "As of this moment, it did," she said. "Guy, you should see what that man can do with a few seeds. It's positively miraculous!"

Guy said softly, "Drink your coffee. The waiter is tired

of bringing hot coffee over here and watching us let it grow cold."

When he took her home, he put his hands on her shoulders and drew her unresisting body to him. He bent his head and his lips touched hers, gently at first, and then with fierce passion. Arleen did not pull away from him, but neither did she respond to his kiss. Finally he let her go.

He said shakily, "Would you consider marrying me?"

"Oh, Guy, I like you very much, but I don't. . . ."

"I know," he said, "you don't love me. I could teach you to love me. Let me take that chance."

"No," Arleen said, "it wouldn't be fair to you. A man and a woman should love each other when they get married." Her voice quivered, "Guy, I wish. . . ."

"No, don't say it." He squeezed her hand. "Two tomorrow afternoon," he said. "And don't build up any false hopes."

Arleen lay awake for a long time that night, staring into the darkness. "Why couldn't I have loved him?" she thought unhappily. "He's one of the very nicest men I know." She closed her eyes. You didn't fall in love with someone because they were nice or because you felt you should, or even because you wanted to.

When she finally did go to sleep, it wasn't Guy Newman who haunted her dreams. It was Mark Wynter.

Arleen phoned Mark before she left for work the next morning. He said, "This guy, is he the one from California you're thinking about marrying?"

"He's the one from California," Arleen told him crisply, "but I've never thought about marrying him! Now, Mark, can you find Peter and have him at Neelie's apartment by two?"

"I'll find him. Rose Luigui should have a pretty good idea of where he can be found."

The morning passed much too slowly for Arleen. When she entered the tenement building on Leland Street, she was waylaid by Rose. Rose's eyes burned with anger and fear. She said, "What are you trying to do to Peter? What's that guy want to talk to him about?"

Arleen said gently, "I'm trying to help him. Mr. Newman is part owner of an airplane factory in California. If he thinks Peter is capable of being trained to work in his factory, he's going to give him a job and train him." Her eyes searched Rose's. "Don't you want Peter to have a chance to get out of Leland Street, away from the Roosters?"

Rose's lips shook. She said fiercely, "If Peter goes away, he'll forget me. I won't mean anything to him!" There was a frightened, unsure, little-girl quality in her voice that touched Arleen's heart, and she almost put out a hand to touch Rose's shoulder. But she knew if she did that the girl would draw back.

Instead, she said softly, "If you really like Peter, Rose, you'll encourage him to have his chance, and trust him not to forget you." She sighed. "If you're talking in terms of adult love, you and Peter are both too young for that. You both should have many boy and girl friends before you settle down to one."

Rose said, with her usual scorn, "Listen, nurse lady, you don't stay young in the slums. You grow up real fast!"

Arleen felt Rose's eyes watch her as she went up the stairs. She felt sorry for the girl. She knew Rose was tortured by the fear of Peter's going away and never seeing her again, but equally by the fear of the Roosters' taking their revenge on him if he stayed.

Guy was already there when she reached Neelie's apartment. He looked around at her entrance and said, "I've been admiring Al's garden. He's quite a man with a bit of dirt and a package of seeds. I never acquired a green thumb."

Neelie said happily from her bed, "He's been telling me all about Capistrano, Miss Anderson. He's seen it, and my, he says, it's really a sight to see."

Guy looked at Arleen and there was the ghost of a grin tugging at his lips.

"Peter Rossi's coming here," Arleen told Neelie. "Mr. Newman is going to talk to him, and maybe he'll give Peter a job in his factory."

Neelie's eyes lit up. "My," she said. "Oh, my, wouldn't that be grand for Peter?" She looked at Guy. "Peter's a good boy," she said. "He ain't bad like some of them around here."

Guy looked at Arleen. "So I've been told," he said. His gaze veered toward the door. "Is this the young man now?"

Arleen looked at Peter, standing in the doorway. He wore the usual uniform, the T-shirt and tight jeans. He had left off the black leather jacket, perhaps, Arleen thought, because he no longer had the right to wear it. An informer would no longer be the leader, nor even a member of the gang.

"Guy," Arleen said, "this is Peter Rossi. Peter, this is Mr. Newman."

"Hi," Peter said, with the faintest lifting of his dark, thick brows.

119

"Peter," Guy said, "let's take a walk. I want to talk to you."

Peter's face was dark with suspicion. "What's the matter with talking right here?"

Guy said crisply, "What's the matter, Peter? Are you afraid to take a walk?"

Peter's face tightened. "Whatta you mean, afraid? I'm not afraid of nobody." He turned around and lunged out of the room ahead of Guy.

Al Ryan said with conviction, "He's a fine man."

Neelie nodded. "A man like that would be good for Peter to know. My, but I hope he gives Peter that job."

Arleen thought, as she sponged and massaged Neelie, "If they don't think I've got *my* fingers crossed, too, they're pretty dumb."

She said to Neelie, "Have you been up today?"

"Just for a minute. Al says I got to do like he tells me." She tossed her husband a grin. "Dr. Wynter was here, and he said if I was real careful maybe in time I might even be walking. With crutches, but walking! Ain't that something to think of? And it was all because of Al. Because I got up, knowing he needed me, and the good Lord gave me the strength to do what I didn't know I could do."

Al shook his head. "You're a crazy woman," he told her. But there was tenderness in his voice.

Guy and Peter were gone for a good half hour. Arleen had finished with Neelie and was repacking her satchel when they returned. She could tell by the look on Guy's face that Peter had come through.

"Well," Guy said, looking at Arleen, "I've hired the first of our new trainees for the plant." He looked around at Peter. "Peter's going to make good. He's got the right stuff in him."

Peter said, sounding awed and confident at one and the same time, "I'm going to night school when I get out there, and get me a high-school diploma. Mr. Newman had to get his high-school diploma that way. He was a slum kid, too."

Rose Luigui's voice shrilled from the doorway, "What about me? I'm supposed to be your girl. You going to just leave me here like I'm dirt?"

Peter went to her. He said, "This is a big chance for me. I've never had a chance before. I'm not going to give it up!" Suddenly he looked hesitant. He glanced at Guy and then at Arleen, and addressed his question between them. "She's right," he said. "I can't just leave her here."

Arleen spoke quickly. "My mother would love to have Rose," she said. "She and my father are all alone now. They live in a small town; it's very pretty in summer, and the people are friendly. There's a nice school in town." She was looking at Rose now, and talking to her. "You could go to school if you wanted, and my mother is a very good cook and seamstress. She could teach you all sorts of things that would come in handy when you have a home of your own. And you'd be safe," she added. "You wouldn't have to be afraid. You could make yourself a completely new life, Rose. It would be up to you."

The girl shook her head vigorously. "If you think I'm going to be a slavey to anyone!"

Arleen said, "My mother and father would treat you as if you were one of their own."

Rose turned fiercely to face Peter. "Why can't I go to California with you?"

"Because I have to be trained for this job," Peter told her. "I won't have enough money to take care of you. I'm going to stay with Mr. Newman until I'm through with my training. After I get settled I could send for you. We could get married." His young voice tightened. "I'm going to make something of myself, Rose. I've got this chance, and I'm going to make good on it. You have a chance, too, and you should want to use it. It wouldn't hurt you to work for Miss Anderson's mother. You could learn from her, and you have a lot to learn, the same as I have."

"You'll forget all about me," she wailed. "California's a long way off."

"We've both got to take that chance, Rose." His lips tightened. "You're an awful fool if you turn down Miss Anderson's offer."

"Peter," she said, her lips trembling, "will you write to me?"

"Sure, I'll write. I'll write every day, if I get the time." He turned his attention to Guy. "There's one thing I've got to attend to first," he said, "and then I'll be ready to leave any time."

Arleen saw the fear cross Rose Luigui's face. Rose said fiercely, "What do you have to do, Peter? Force a fight with the Roosters? Prove how brave you are?"

"If I went without forcing Lonnie to a showdown for what he did, they'd say I sneaked away; I was too chicken to stay."

"What do you care what they think?"

Peter put her aside gently. He said, looking not at her but at Guy Newman, "This is something I have to do."

Guy nodded. When the door had closed behind Peter, he said, "Peter has to live with himself."

CHAPTER 20

THE NIGHT came on swiftly; the lights glowed in the windows along the streets. Arleen stood looking out the window of her apartment, thinking. She was unutterably weary and tense. She had phoned her mother the moment she'd come home. Both she and her father had insisted they would be happy to have Rose Luigui.

Arleen had to warn them, "She's sullen and defiant. She isn't like any child you've ever known."

Her mother laughed softly. "I think I can cope with her, dear. When in doubt, I always apply love in large doses."

Evelyn, reading a magazine, legs sprawled over the side of the large armchair, said, "What are you so restless about? You've solved your Leland Street problems, haven't you? Peter and the Ryans go to California, Rose to your mother's. What have you got to fret about now?"

"I'm worried over Peter," Arleen said. "He insisted on having a showdown with this Lonnie Michos who's taken over the Roosters."

"Mark would have phoned you if something had happened to Peter."

Arleen said, "Maybe nothing has happened yet; maybe they're biding their time." She drew a deep breath, went into the bedroom and combed her hair for the nth time.

Evelyn was right, and she should be happy over the way everything had turned out. Neelie was getting her dream, both for herself and for Al.

Neelie had said happily, "Mr. Newman says next year Al can drive me to Capistrano and I can be there when the swallows return." Her eyes had glowed. "Didn't I tell you," she said to Arleen, "that everyone has this big chunk of happiness coming to them? Well, this here's Al's and my big chunk."

Arleen could see that Guy was as drawn to Neelie as she'd been.

Al had objected bitterly when Guy first offered him the job. His pride had sounded in his voice. "You don't have to go giving me anything, Mr. Newman!"

"I don't intend to," Guy had told him curtly. "I didn't make the few dollars I have by giving things away to people. If I'm paying you to work for me, I'll expect plenty of work in return. If you aren't satisfactory I won't keep you on. No favors."

Al had nodded, satisfied. Arleen had seen the new straightening of his shoulders. "Fair enough," he'd said.

"We're going to have a house," Neelie had marveled, "a real house, with four rooms in it! My, me and Al have never had four rooms of our own in our married life!"

As she remembered Neelie's childlike happiness at the miracle that had happened to her, some of the heaviness lifted from Arleen's heart.

She was walking out of the bedroom when the phone rang.

Mark's voice was cheerful and hopeful. "Peter made his play," he said. "He saw, he fought, he conquered." He ended on a serious note. "For the time being, that is."

Arleen gripped the phone. "What happened, Mark?"

"Peter played it smart. He waited until Lonnie had only a couple of the Roosters with him, and then he challenged him. He accused him of insulting Rose, and of beating up Al Ryan. He said that a boy who curled his hair was too chicken to pick on someone his own size and sex. He said Lonnie wouldn't fight unless he had a knife or a gang to back him up. He walked up to Lonnie and slapped him across the face."

Mark seemed to find delight in the telling. "I had a front-row seat. Lonnie Michos flung insults back at Peter, but he wouldn't fight him. Not with his bare hands, he wouldn't. Peter walked away from there as if he'd won a fight in the ring. He did win today, but it's not over, Arleen. The next time Peter won't win. Out in the open isn't how these kids fight. They don't know the rules of that kind of fighting."

Arleen said, "Mark, Peter has the job with Guy. He's going to California to work. And Neelie and Al Ryan are going too! Al is going to take care of Guy's lawn, and the lawn at the factory, and do janitor work. Neelie is certain miracles can and do happen!"

"Well," Mark said, "that leaves only Rose Luigui, doesn't it?"

"Oh, Rose is taken care of, too. She's going to stay with

my mother. My mother isn't young any longer, and she can use someone to help out."

Mark made a sound in his throat. "Angel of Leland Street," he said. "I guess you do deserve the title, Arleen."

"Oh, Mark, don't be silly!"

He said, "I have some news too. I'm moving into offices downtown. I'm going to keep my offices down here, and practise here evenings."

Arleen said softly, "I can help you if you'd like, Mark. I hardly do anything with my evenings."

"You should have all of your evenings taken, a girl as pretty as you are." And then he added, with boyish humor, "But I'm glad you don't."

Peter Rossi wore a new shirt, sports jacket and slacks. "Mr. Newman treated me to the clothes," he told Arleen. His jaw tightened. "I'm paying him back, though. He understands that."

Neelie was radiant. And Al Ryan looked a good ten years younger, Arleen thought. "It's just like it's a dream," Neelie kept saying. "I ain't been so happy since the day Al asked me to marry him." She twinkled at her husband. "Maybe you'll come out to California on your honeymoon," she told Arleen.

Arleen, aware of Mark close by, within listening range, said quickly, "I'm not planning any honeymoon, Neelie. Nor wedding, either."

"You will be, one of these days," Neelie said serenely.

Arleen saw Rose and Peter standing off to one side. They were talking quietly, their hands tightly clasped. Rose was crying. She was still crying, quietly and openly, when Peter walked her to the train, which was getting ready to pull out.

"I ain't forgetting you had a lot to do with me getting this chance," Peter told Arleen. He grinned, looking suddenly boyish. "Maybe next time you see me I won't be saying 'ain't.' "

"Write to me, Peter," Rose said, anxiously.

"I told you I would. I'm going to work hard, and you do the same," he told Rose. He grinned again. "I don't want you spouting 'ain't' either, the next time I see you!"

There was one other train to catch. Rose Luigui was taking the train north to Carson. Anna Luigui, when approached for permission for Rose to leave home, had shrugged. "So she leaves. Who cares? All she does here is

124

nag, nag, and fight with her mama. I be glad when she's gone. An ungrateful daughter. A bad daughter!"

Miss Gibbons had thought it a good move for Rose. She didn't have much hope that Rose would show any gratitude, however. Her coldish eyes studied Arleen's face. "You really have hope these people are going to help themselves, don't you? That they're going to hold onto their jobs, and make good?"

It wasn't a question but a statement. Then she shrugged. "Well, I suppose miracles do sometimes happen."

Arleen, thinking of Neelie, nodded. "Yes," she said, softly, "they do happen, Miss Gibbons."

At the last moment Rose almost backed out. She said unhappily, "What about Carmella and Angela and Pietro? What about them?"

Arleen said quietly, "Angela is getting big enough to do things for the younger children, Rose. If you take this chance and make good, maybe you'll be the one to give Angela her chance. And perhaps Pietro and Carmella."

"I don't know why Ma ever had kids," Rose said fiercely. "She don't take care of them. She don't love them. They don't know what that word is!"

Arleen said, "You know, Rose. You can teach them. You can teach them the good things of life. But first you have to take your chance. Without it you're no good to them or to yourself." Her voice softened. "And Peter is depending on you."

Rose said unhappily, "Will he write to me? Will he forget me?"

Arleen shook her head. "He won't forget you, and he'll write." Her eyes swept the girl's face. "You and Peter," she said, "know what the bad times are like, Rose. Now it's time you learned that life can be good, too."

As the train got ready to pull out, Rose suddenly reached out a hand and held Arleen's tightly. She said unsteadily, "I'm scared. I'm scared. I can't do it! I can't!"

It was the first time the girl had turned toward Arleen, and there was a warmth in Arleen's heart. "You don't have to be afraid," she said. "And you can do whatever you want to, Rose. You'll like my mother and father. They know what love is; they taught me about it when I was a little girl. Look up, dear. Look up."

She was still waving as the train pulled out. She stepped back, and then was aware of Mark beside her. She said anxiously, "Will she go through with it, Mark? Everything

125

is going to be strange and hard for her at first. Will she have the courage?"

"Human nature is unpredictable, but I'd say that if your parents have any of your qualities . . . and since they are your parents, I judge they do have . . . Rose will be given all of the incentive she needs to enable her to make good. And besides, there's Peter. Rose is smart enough to know that she can't stand still and let Peter climb above her. Not if she wants to keep him, she can't."

Suddenly he bent toward Arleen. "I love you," he said.

Arleen shivered at his touch. They were in a railroad station; people milled around them, but it was as if they were completely alone.

"I love you, too, Mark," Arleen said. She was amazed at how simple it was to say. She had told Rose, "Look up." That went for her, too. Johnny was a wound that had long since healed. She was no longer afraid of love; it was a glory within her.

"I can't offer you luxuries," Mark said. "I can't even offer you a decent living. Everyone is going to tell you that you're crazy to marry a dedicated man. And they'll be right. But I love you. That's all I have to offer." .

"It's enough," Arleen said, the love throbbing in her voice. "And I'm a dedicated woman, too, Mark. I can't give up my nursing. I wouldn't want to."

"I wouldn't ask you to." Mark bent to kiss her. The kiss went on and on. Someone coughed, and Mark raised his head. He said, his voice shaky from the kiss, "Good heavens, do you realize we're putting on a show?"

Arleen laughed. It didn't matter. Nothing mattered except that Mark loved her, and she loved him. And the fear in her was completely gone.

Mark said, "I guess we'd better come back to reality and realize we both still have patients to care for."

Arleen nodded. "Mark," she said, "we've found a way out for four of them, but what about the others?"

Mark touched her nose with a fingertip. "Remember when I told you that if you succeeded in finding a way out for even one you'd accomplished a lifetime of work? You have to be satisfied with little." He bent to kiss her again. "Don't forget you're promised," he told her, "and don't let anyone talk you out of doing this crazy thing!"

Arleen laughed. "I always enjoyed doing crazy things, Mark." Her voice was soft as a kiss. "And I could never, never forget I was promised to you."

Evelyn shook her head when Arleen told her she was going to marry Mark. "I think you're crazy," she said, hugging her. "But I hope you'll be very, very happy with your dedicated doctor."

The telegram from Guy Newman arrived at seven o'clock. "Going back to California," it said. "I don't mind bumping my head against a stone wall, as long as I figure I can make a breakthrough. But I've seen your doctor, and I know the stone wall's too tough. If you change your mind, look me up. Don't worry about your protégés. They're my protégés, too. Love. Wish it were on both sides. Guy."

Arleen had a moment of sadness. And then she thought, "Guy is a young man. He'll find someone else, a girl who will love him as he deserves to be loved."

The sadness didn't last long. When you're in love and know you are loved in return, and the future stretches ahead of you like a radiant promise, it is very hard to be anything except happy.

And Arleen Anderson was aglow with happiness, like a rose that has at last reached full blooming.